KARSTEN KREPINSKY
New Berlin: The Children of Icarus

Translated from the German by
KARIN DUFNER

Karsten Krepinsky
New Berlin: The Children of Icarus

Copyright (c) 2022/2023 by Dr. Karsten Krepinsky, Berlin
Original German edition, January 2023
English translation in March 2023 by Karin Dufner
www.karindufner.de
All rights reserved
Reprints and reproductions (also in parts) with the author's written permission only
Cover design by Ingo Krepinsky, Die TYPONAUTEN
www.typonauten.de/eng
Copy-editing: Ursula and Ingo Krepinsky
Printed and published by BoD – Books on Demand, Norderstedt
ISBN: 978-3734721731
Berlin, April 2023

www.theworldbehindthewindow.com

About the Book

Sometime in the remote future. The acrid smell of burning fires has settled over the City of New Berlin. Billowing smoke obscures the sun. The city itself has been under siege for twenty years by now, everything but its very center being under enemy control. A military regime uses rigid oppression to make its citizens toe the line. Dissenters and collaborators are weeded out by an army of headhunters. Max Hofstetter is one of them. When his immediate boss, Charlotte Fleming, orders him to bring down the killer of a high-ranking government official, his search leads him into the Forbidden Zone, as the area that surrounds Berlin's TV tower now is called. When the discovery of the leadership's most closely guarded secret rocks his world, the hunter is turned into prey…

A Science-Fiction Thriller

About the Author

Dr. Karsten Krepinsky lives in Berlin where he works for a startup as a biologist in the field of neuroscience. His second passion is publishing novels as a freelance writer. The many facets and diversities of Berlin, Germany's capital, never cease to serve as inspirations for his thrillers, which include elements of sci-fi, mystery, and horror.

For my mother

Brick's Map of the New Berlin Cauldron

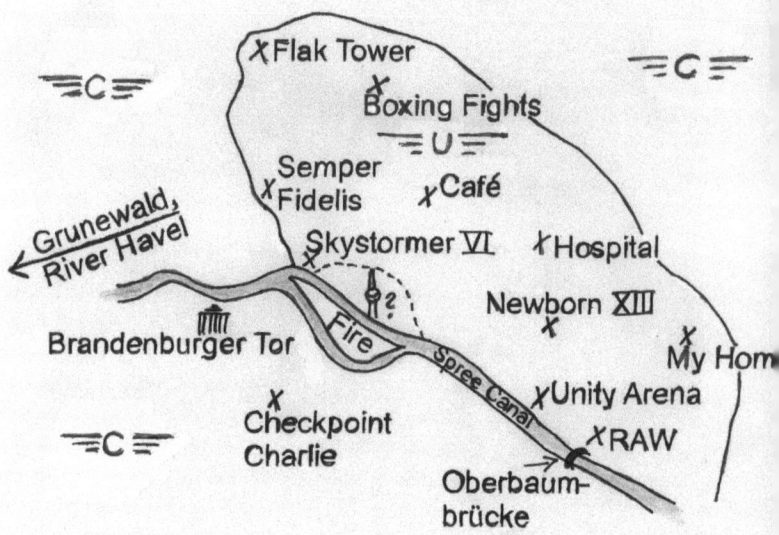

Prologue

I need to wait for the right moment to strike. The man first, then the woman. If I don't make a mistake, they both don't stand a chance. Four thrusts with my bayonet will be enough to do the job. What I can't get my head around is the question why the two of them are in such high spirits. They sit at the bank of the canal, clinking glasses, as if they hadn't a care in the world. Why this festive mood? I can hardly wait to crash their little party. All I need to do is bid my time.

1
New Berlin, Oberbaumbrücke

The facades of New Berlin look as if someone had covered them with a layer of wax. Windows and doors have long vanished under a viscous mass of oil, gunk, and some indefinable fungous lichen. A cloud of dense smoke darkens the sky day and night. The presence of the sun can only be assumed. I'm standing on Oberbaumbrücke, gazing down into the dry river bed underneath the bridge. The Spree, once a wide river, meandering slowly through the City of Berlin, has meanwhile turned into a dusty trench. The silhouettes of the skyscrapers at Alexanderplatz form a stark contrast to a raging ocean of fire. The eternal flame at the Olympic Stadium has long died, but is now wreaking havoc on Museumsinsel. The enemy has set fire to one of the five subterranean fuel depots we have installed there before the siege.

When you divide the area inside New Berlin's ring road into four sections, the north-eastern wedge belongs to us. We control the boroughs of Friedrichshain, Prenzlauer Berg, and the eastern part of Mitte with an iron fist. In Kreuzberg, however, we just manage to maintain a toehold, as the enemy has progressed all the way to Schlesisches Tor. Thudding detonations are a constant reminder of the war raging in the sub-level, where we have engaged the enemy in a merciless battle.

We have to keep up resistance until reinforcements arrive. I'm aware of this. I'm a patriot and I love my country. But I still want to tell the truth. That's what I've sworn to myself, when I came across this old-fashioned dictating machine. I will neither conceal nor gloss over anything. Lies and malice are already rampant in this city, which has been a war-zone for two decades now. When I found the dictating machine, my first impulse was to destroy it, because the law says so. Keeping records is not allowed, lest they fall into the enemy's hands, revealing our weak spots and the doubts that plague us, which will then be used against us. I'm a patriot. They are not supposed to get hold of anything that might help them. However, I'm skeptical when I think of our mission. What kind of future will we have, when we annihilate our own past?

As hardly anyone comes out here, I can finally be just myself. In the sub-level, the motto is strictly *we* and *us*. No exceptions. But as much as I like to seek safety in numbers, I just love these quiet moments up here. There's no such thing as a free lunch, though, and the price is high to spend time in this hostile cityscape just to stare at a dusty river bed. My urge to cough is growing stronger by the moment. It's not recommended to stay outside for more than thirty minutes at a time. The houses are all sealed. An intricate network of hatches brings you down to the sub-level, the next entrance being less than fifteen feet away. Just a couple of soldiers are patrolling the streets. There is no one else around.

2
Riding the Subway, Line U257

REMEMBER, the legend on the doors of the subway car says. The inscription is everywhere. And everyone knows what it means: Remember who we are. Keep in mind who our enemy is. And never forget what we're fighting for. I hide the dictating machine in my pocket, away from prying eyes. Everything happens for a reason, I'm absolutely certain. The cars of the magnetic train gather speed when we get to a straight stretch in the tracks. The city of New Berlin is veined with subway lines like the tissue of a muscle; those trains being the only way to get from A to B. A man with a scar on his cheek is staring at me. He proudly wears a badge on his beret: the golden cross for bravery with the red heart of the disabled veteran. The man clutches the grab pole with his prosthetic arm. There's hardly anyone aboard the train who doesn't have some kind of war injury. I'm one of the few who appear unharmed. From the outside, that is. Just looking at me, you would never guess. It's my brain that has been affected.

Sometimes I see myself sitting at the bank of River Spree. It's a picnic, I think. When did it take place? No idea. The dense fog that shrouds my memory never lifts. Suddenly, the subway cars come to a halt. I've arrived at my destination. The guy in the wheelchair who gets out before me reminds me of the picnics on the banks of River Spree that will never happen anymore. Not today. Not tomorrow.

The U-Atrium at Helmholtzplatz is the nicest one we have. The builders of these public meeting places have done an excellent job, recreating urban life underground. From the spouting fountain in the center, small waterways spread in a radial to the stores that make up the shopping mall. The gurgling of the water has a soothing effect on people. Water is precious. Once a year, during the rainy season, we collect the rainwater we'll need during the long months of drought.

I need to shield my eyes when I raise them to the U-Atrium's dome. The glare of the floodlights and ceiling lamps is blinding. Nothing happens without a reason. Doesn't finding the dictating machine mean that it's my job to record my thoughts? Dust has settled on the buildings of New Berlin, covering up the past. Like a living organism, the city is subject to constant changes. The setting has been altered, while the people in it have remained the same. REMEMBER. Remember who we are. What we are fighting for. And who our enemies are. We need to remember. I need to remember.

3

Café "Spreeblick" on the Shopping-Mall's Gallery, U-Atrium Helmholtzplatz, Sub-Level 1

"Have you been outside again?" Charlotte joins me at my table. The dirt on my coat doesn't escape her. "What are you looking for up there?" she wants to know, sitting down beside me. The soldiers at the next table are loud and boisterous. The fresh bandages on their arms and legs tell me that they've just come from the front. "The polluted air... how do you stand it?" Charlotte frowns. "The human body isn't made for this." Her pancake-makeup can't hide the heavy wrinkles. Charlotte Fleming has been a beautiful woman once, but the decades of war have prematurely aged her. She's wearing a support corset, which she adjusts whenever she thinks I'm not looking. Now, she's shaking her head disapprovingly. "The war doesn't seem to bother you in the least, Brick." Her statement sounds like an accusation. Brick is the nickname I've acquired since my accident. Even though it wasn't a brick that hit me on the head.

Charlotte is the chief of the Secret Police, and I'm her most senior headhunter. At least that's what she always claims, insisting that I'm the best bloodhound she's ever had. I don't know if it's true. Maybe Charlotte just wants to flatter me.
"What can I get you?" The waitress is looking down on us. She smoothes her hair off her perfectly symmetrical face with one hand. Her name-tag says

"Felicitas"—the happy one. The name tells it all. She's kept her body in good shape. Her cheeks redden, when she looks at me.

Charlotte is eyeing her skeptically. "Today's special," she tersely says.

"And what would you like to have?" Felicitas gives me an expectant smile, while twirling a blonde tress between her fingers.

I don't need to think. "Yellow, if you please."

"We're having blue weeks, variation green," Felicitas replies.

"Oh, how stupid of me... I forgot." Our choices consist of blue, red, and yellow jellies. Mixed in different ratios. "In this case get me blue please, blue like the ocean."

"Green for me," Charlotte says.

The waitress smiles at me before taking off.

My eyes follow her for a moment. "You have anything for me?"

Charlotte clears her throat. "Do you know the antique shop 'Before Our Times' in the U-Atrium at Frankfurter Tor?"

"Of course I do. I live nearby."

"There was a murder in the place."

"A murder?" I'm getting curious.

"Do you know the owner?"

"Just in passing."

The waitress arrives with our order. Charlotte can't make up her mind whether to direct her disdain against the beautiful Felicitas or the green Jell-O-like substance, wobbling on her plate. Just shoot the messenger. Even if the message comes in the guise of lousy food. And even if the server is called Felicitas.

Charlotte is picking at her jelly, obviously not wanting it. "What's your business in an antique shop?"

"Looking for antiques."

"What exactly are you looking for?"

"My past."

"You're not that old."

"Forty-one. Just like you."

Charlotte puts down her fork and leans back in her chair. "You're still having memory problems?"

"The doctor tells me to get myself a hobby. Sooner or later the memories will return."

"What about Paul Bull?"

"What about him?"

"You need something to occupy you, and I'm giving you a name. Paul Bull, the owner of 'Before Our Times'."

"I know who Paul Bull is. Why do you mention his name?"

"Take a guess."

"Is Bull the victim?"

"Looks like it." Charlotte averts her eyes. She has been watching me the entire time. "We need to know who liquidated him."

This is a case I'd rather stay clear of. I don't like the idea to turn the antique shop upside down. "You're sure it was murder?"

"You don't get bullet holes from falling on your face," Charlotte scoffs. "Go to the store and have a look around. If you still don't like the case when you're through, I'll pull you off."

"Do your people still hang out there?"

"Don't you worry about my boys."

"I'm a headhunter, not an investigator."

"My men simply lack your talent, Brick. Yes, they're well trained, but you have the... knack for it. You need to solve this case for me."

"That'll be 50,000 Credits."

"You must be joking."

"That's the amount I need."

"What for?"

"You know, what for."

Charlotte's laugh is full of contempt. "For your therapy?"

"I want my memories back." I massage my temples with circular movements. "The answers to my questions are in there, somewhere inside my head."

Wolfing down the jelly is a matter of seconds for Charlotte. Food is just a necessity for her to keep the vital functions going. "Find us the killer, then I'll see what I can do for you."

"I'll do my best."

"What is it you're looking for in your past? I just don't get it." Charlotte is gazing at me. "Maybe you won't like what you find."

The soldiers at the next table are leaving the café in a hurry. Loud voices resound in the atrium. Charlotte and I follow the soldiers to the mall's gallery. Before we take off, Charlotte has her eyes scanned by the intercom. These consoles are linked to the central computer and are installed in all public and private areas. "My treat." Two credits are deducted from Charlotte's bank account. She can afford it.

"Bastards!" somebody is hollering. In front of the café an angry crowd has gathered. "These fucking bastards!" One soldier raises his fist in a threatening gesture. Now, I see the reason behind the turmoil. Someone has sprayed the red letter "C" on the front of the café. Not a smart idea. Every nook and cranny of the mall is covered by cameras. Identifying the culprit shouldn't be too much of a problem for the Observators in the Control Center. "U! U! U!" people aggressively chant. One soldier aims a glob of saliva at the graffiti. "Universals!" he screams. "We're Universals!" He beats his chest with his fists. Charlotte takes my hand. It feels like an electric shock. Then, she smiles for the first time this day. More and more people reach out for each other's hands, and it takes only seconds to form a human chain. "U! U! U!" I join in. It doesn't make a difference that I can't remember. Because I'm shoulder to shoulder with everyone else, fighting for my comrades. "Unity! Unity! Unity!" The red "C" stands for the *others*. It's *us* and *them*. And it's them, who started the war. "U! U! U!" we're chanting as one. The Colonials won't be able to break our unity. It's a mixture of hatred and bliss that fills my entire being. "U! U! U!"

4

Antique Shop 'Before Our Times', U-Atrium Frankfurter Tor, Sub-Level 1

There's only a viscous mass on the carpet, where I expected to find Bull's body. Putrefaction must have been well advanced. Three bullets are embedded in the wall. This means the murder weapon was a firearm, an important detail, as pistols and rifles are hard to come by. For spies and assassins, knives, hammers, and axes are the usual weapons of choice. It makes me wonder why the killer hasn't opted for the quiet way. Is the MO supposed to convey a message? I eye the iron grill, separating the store proper from the area behind the counter. The angle in which the shot was fired across the entire store tells me that the perpetrator must have been inside the place. And to enter the store, you have to be admitted by Bull. If I draw the right conclusions from the track marks on the carpet, Bull didn't die at once, but dragged himself across the floor for a number of feet, before life left him.

"What do you want, Brick?" The vice-chief of the Secret Police jams his hands into his coat pockets. As I have feared, Jeremiah Glass and his team are still at the scene. The backs of their black trench coats are emblazoned with the acronym P.I.D.: Police of Inner Defense. Glass is a living legend. A face prosthesis shimmers through the long hair of his wig. Half of his face has been torn off by an explosive device, disfiguring him on the day of the grand spring offensive, when West City was lost to the Colonials. They say Glass stopped the enemy's attack inside the U-Atrium at Schlesisches Tor by fending off the aggressors all by himself until enforcements arrived. The legend has it that he butchered thirty enemy soldiers in hand-to-hand combat. This was five years ago. Now and then, Glass's customized prosthesis gets dislodged, emitting a noise that almost sounds like a toaster popping slices of bread. Therefore, his nickname is Toaster.

Toaster cultivates the image of being a creep. The idea behind it is not so much scaring suspects during interrogations, but to make his subordinates quake in their boots. When I look at the men who have come with him to the scene today, it's quite obvious that they keep their distance to the boss, whom they all seem to be in awe of. Toaster has survived a number of attempts on his life. The doctors so far have always managed to patch him up again.

I wipe my parched lips. "Where is Bull's corpse?"

"Let's put it this way, we've scraped up what was left of him with shovels and shipped it off to the morgue in a body bag."

"With shovels? Care to share any details?"

When Toaster smiles a grim smile, only the right corner of his mouth goes up. This is all I get for an answer. I go down on my knees to take a closer look at the stains on the carpet. The outline corresponds with that of an overweight, tall man. Which again matches Bull's built. "The body must have been here for days," I say. I hear a click that resembles a toaster popping bread. The smell of coffee is in the air. When have I had my last slice of toast? In another lifetime, it seems. A sweet deception. Scent is the most powerful sense of memory we have.

Toaster clicks his facial prosthesis back into place. The crack between the two halves of his face disappears. He seems to bask in the attention this little ritual affords him. "The murder happened less than five hours ago."

"Impossible!" I point my finger at the body liquids that have seeped all the way into the pile of the cotton rug.

"Careful with the premature conclusions." Toaster's smile again lifts the right corner of his mouth only, giving his face a disturbingly asymmetrical appearance. "He was a Speedy."

"Speedy...," I repeat, incredulously shaking my head. That some bodies seem to dissolve to goo in almost no time, decaying more or less on fast-forward, is a persistent urban myth. I'm not a believer. I rather go for facts. I eye Toaster's gun holster. The members of the Secret Police carry arms.

Toaster covers his belt buckle with his trench coat to hide the gun. Knowing that there is a spy among the ranks of the P.I.D. must be a nightmare for Toaster. "Bull used his intercom six hours ago," Toaster now says.

"Are you sure that it was Bull himself?" I walk over to the intercom and activate the console above the iris scanner. The communications platform opens at once. The intercom seems to work just fine. "Maybe someone started using Bull's eye? Just his eye, I mean."

"Don't you know that the scanner can tell dead eyes apart from live ones?"

"Yeah, I know, artery control. But it's possible to override it." I've heard of iris scanners activated with eyes that had been separated from their bodies before. "What about the surveillance cam in the store?" I inquire.

"The killer was a pro." Toaster points at the camera above the counter.

I notice the paint someone has sprayed on the lens. It's red. The same color as the graffitied "C" on the façade of Café Spreeblick in the U-Atrium at Helmholtzplatz.

"We'd better leave Brick alone. Maybe he'll find something we didn't." Toaster gives a disdainful laugh. "Let's split!" The P.I.D. men obey wordlessly. I know that Toaster will analyze the recordings of the cameras in the vicinity of the store to see who has walked in. Which could turn out to create problems for me.

The dictating machine I use to record my thoughts was bought in this very antique shop. I step into the next room, which is separated from the shop floor with a curtain. Here, Bull used to store his most valuable pieces. Sooner or later Toaster will find out that I was a regular here. I might be on his list of suspects already. Charlotte's questioning looks during our meeting at the café have not escaped me. I don't have much time to flush out the killer, before I end up on the hit list myself.

I take a dirty rag off a chest that sits in a corner of the storage room. "Icarus" says the writing on its lid. According to Bull he bought the chest from one of the so called Diggers, who work for him. Diggers are treasure hunters and operate free-lance, like headhunters do. They are the only ones who dare venture down into the crumbling sub-levels deep in the underbelly of the city, where the most valuable artifacts can be found. Only a few of those Diggers ever return from their forays into this netherworld.

A thudding sound attracts my attention. When I take a peep into the store proper, I realize what's going on. Someone is hiding in the shaft of the air conditioning system. When I yank off the grid, I'm met by a stare from blue eyes. My reflexes are too slow.

When I come to, my chest hurts. I run my fingers across my coat und finally pull a syringe from my chest. The drug I was injected with must have paralyzed me in a matter of seconds. I try to reconstruct what has happened. The person who tricked me was a woman. She must have overheard my conversation with Toaster. Who knows how long she'd been lurking in the air conditioning shaft. I'm still not steady on my feet, when I stumble over to the storage room. Why did the woman let me live? The chest in the store room has been opened, the artifact kept inside it is gone. The woman must have stolen it.

Is she also Bull's killer? When I look over to the intercom, my vision blurs and I'm having problems to focus. I massage my eyelids in an attempt to see clearer. I feel sick like from a hangover. According to the clock on the intercom I've been out for twenty minutes. I check my flashlight. The battery is charged. I shine the lamp into the shaft. Iron rungs lead down into the abyss. I can make out fresh footprints in the layer of rust that covers them. The woman was blonde and had blue eyes and high cheekbones. She also had a scar on her chin. There's no time to lose. I have to get her.

5
U-Atrium RAW, Sub-Level 1

In the clubs and brothels of U-Atrium RAW shady characters abound. River Spree is nearby; its opposite bank is under enemy control. We are very close to the front, where an odd mixture of hedonism and apocalypse rules. The result is a chaotic mingling of human bodies, which would make it easy for the woman to get lost in the crowd. Judging by the traces I found she must have left the shaft somewhere inside Club Cassiopeia.

The rooms in the upper floors of Cassiopeia are bathed in a murky light. I pass sofas where men and women vegetate, blearily staring into space with eyes half open. In a side room, a rotating illumination sphere casts thousands of points of light onto the ceiling. Everyone here is on some intoxicating substance or the other. Some are sniffing cheap glue, while others still have enough Credits to inject themselves with *Illusion*. Lost souls, all of them. Most of the time we don't bother these Outsiders, as their turn to pay their dues will come up soon enough. In case of an offensive, Outsiders are used as cannon fodder and sent into the first rows to trigger booby traps.

"Hey, Brick, what have you been doing with yourself? You're all sweaty and dirty." Cassiopeia's manager comes up to greet me. Claus Schwarzkopf, called Cassio by everyone, wears inked "U"s on his neck and forehead. And who knows, what other body parts he had tattooed. It's not my thing to show my loyalties this way. Patriotism is a matter of the heart. "You need to clean out your ventilation shaft," I joke.

"Ventilation shaft?" Cassio frowns at me. "Do you mean that you...? What's wrong with the door?"

"After the little encounter I had last time, I'd rather not bump into your doormen again."

Cassio laughs. The next moment his face darkens. "What do you want, Brick?"

"I'm looking for a blonde."

"Almost all my ladies are blondes."

"And what about a scar?"

"Scar?"

"I'm looking for a blonde with a scar on her chin. It's about two and a half inches long."

Cassio eyes me suspiciously. "If I happen to bump into a woman with a scar, I'll let you know."

I'm thrown out of the club without having seen the woman, all the while wondering, why she has run to RAW of all places. It's a dead end here. Almost all subway tunnels are blocked. The only one still in use leads to our last outpost in the borough of Kreuzberg.

Two companies of marines are waiting on the platform. They'll relieve the troops at the front line. In the corner of my eye I see a figure scuttling across the platform, the hood of her parka drawn deep into her face. Warning signals announce the arrival of a train. Is she the woman with the scar? I need to make up my mind. The doors are already closing when I hop aboard the train.

The marines are standing shoulder to shoulder. The woman must be about five doors down the car. This time I came prepared. Feeling for my harpoon-gun, I push through the throng of soldiers. The marines complain, but let me pass. The light in the car stars flickering. The train slows down and finally comes to a halt. We haven't reached U-Atrium Schlesisches Tor yet. Through the crowd of soldiers, I catch a glimpse of a woman wearing an anorak. She's frantically trying to force open the door. I pull my gun from the shoulder holster and take aim. The catching loop is coiled, the weapon ready to fire. She'll be my catch no. 98. The woman turns around and looks into my eyes. It's now or never. I pull the trigger.

The lights go off. "They've broken through," a corporal whispers. "The Colonials have broken through."
"Come on! Everyone out into the tunnel!" the major orders. When the doors of the car are pushed open, the soldiers erupt onto the tracks. I try to withdraw into a corner of the car, but get pushed over. Emergency lighting clicks on. I see that the dart of my harpoon has tacked the woman's anorak to the wall of the car. The woman herself got away. She must have pulled free at the last moment. I pick myself up, yank the dart from the wall and jump from the train.

"They're coming!" A soldier, his face bloodied, is running at me in panic. He must be coming from the outpost at Schlesisches Tor. "Get away, idiot!" he screams at me. The tunnel reverberates from the echo of thudding footsteps. The enemy is near.

"Defense formation!" the major barks. The two companies take position in front of the train. Just in time. The Squeezers make up the first row, bearing the brunt of the attack. They are the tallest and strongest among our soldiers. Their body armors protect them from the Colonials' stabs. Screams and groans are accompanied by the clanging of sickle blades, when the Cutters on both sides attempt to cut a swathe through the formation. A bloody job, perfectly choreographed and staged in a gruesome performance. I help the Pullers who attempt to separate individual fighters from their comrades. Someone stabs at my arm, but it's just a flesh wound. With joint forces we manage to pull a Colonial out of the first row of the attackers. He's a very strong man. Four of us need to cling on to his arms and legs to drag him behind the lines. But all his thrashing is in vain. With a deft flick of his hand, the major pulls the helmet off the Colonial scum's head and knocks him out with his club.

A female soldier approvingly slaps my shoulder. I know her. Her name is Eva. We both laugh. I look at her bloody uniform. We are companions in fate. Tough and defiant. My blood blends with that of my brothers and sisters. We will hold up until the siege is broken. The Marines in the first line are screaming with joy: "U! U! U!" The Colonials start to draw back.

"U! U! U!" Our voices join in a tremendous chorus. "Unity! Unity! Unity!" Eva hugs me. We're alive. I pull Eva to my chest and kiss her, tasting the blood coming from her mouth.

6
The Next Morning
Residential Depots "Samariterstrasse", Friedrichshain, Sub-Level 1

The last time I saw Eva, she wasn't with the Storm Troops yet. This was six months ago. Eva was living with a Supervisor in Prenzlauer Berg, sharing a place in a residential tower close to Mauerpark. Not in a sub-level like me, but at top-level with a view of New Berlin—if you want to call looking at a city shrouded in smoke a view. The privileges Supervisors enjoy are an issue some people gripe about, if no one is listening. The extra food packages, the luxury top-level apartments, the special compartments when they travel by subway. I, however, don't mind all these things. Supervisors bear the brunt of responsibility for our community after all. It's their job to make everyone comply with the universal rules.

I'm not interested in luxury anyway. My simple sleeping cubicle is more than enough for me. About one hundred square feet, bed, bathroom unit, table. Food is delivered once a day via tube mail. It's not much, but sufficient. I also don't need a panoramic window to take a look at New Berlin. If I want to risk a peek, I just go outside. A little coughing fit won't kill me. Unfiltered, dirty air, that's what reality is like. I'll never get a total grasp of the city I live in, when I stay behind the windows of an apartment, where my lungs are filled with fresh filtered air.

Eva is next to me in bed. The blood of yesterday's battle still smears her cheek. I moisten my finger to wipe off the stain, and kiss her. Eva is thirty-eight and thinks that she can hear her biological clock ticking away. Did she shack up with the Supervisor to increase her odds for a baby? I only met her boyfriend once. He was in his sixties, like all Supervisors are. Maybe he couldn't do anything for her. Eva didn't want to tell me what drove her to join the Marines. But there's testosterone aplenty among the Storm Troopers, that much is clear.

Are there still children being born inside the cauldron? To the rest of us little ones have become something like fabled beings from a faraway past. If there still are minors around, the Supervisors do their best to hide them away. Due to a quirk of nature, most of us happen to be around the same age. Twenty years ago, just before the ring around New Berlin was closed, there was a mass-evacuation, leaving only men and women of fighting age behind. This is what they tell us, at least. I've no idea what really happened back then as my memories of the time before the siege are vague. Sometimes I feel like a castaway sailor. Stranded on a desert island, surrounded by an ocean of oblivion.

Eva's fast asleep. I can't remember how long it's been since I slept through the night the last time. It is as if my mind were afraid of dreaming. I stare at the dripping faucet. Twenty years are a long time. The infrastructure is crumbling away. We will prevail until reinforcements arrive. However, I can't tell how much of New Berlin will be left by then. I remove the bandage from my arm and take a look at the cut. The gel worked just fabulously, the wound has almost mended. If only every wound would heal as easily. We inhabitants of the cauldron are all in our early forties. I need to trust our Supervisors. They've helped us through every crisis so far. Death, however, is something even Supervisors can't do anything about. Age is a currency. Our time is running out.

I walk to the intercom to scan my iris. 10,000 Credits have been added to my account. Charlotte has made the first deposit. It's more generous than usual. But payment also means that there is work awaiting me. I'm expected to deliver. A message pops up in my mailbox. Charlotte wants to meet me in the Volksbühne. I have an hour left. Maybe Eva and I can have breakfast together. A bleep tells me that the food has arrived. Exactly on time, like it always does. I unscrew the capsule. A portion of yellow jelly. The colors change every week. I like yellow. It reminds me of the sun.

7
Volksbühne at Rosa-Luxemburg-Platz, Sub-Level 1

The U-Hall is filled to the last seat. I stand with Charlotte on the balcony. Charlotte really seems to be impressed with me. She also seems to have plans for me, even though I've no idea what they might be. Like always, I feel certain distance between us, which she is careful to maintain. The light man aims the spotlight at the lectern. Matthäus Stegner, one of the most senior Supervisors, will address the Community. "I know that many of you harbor doubts," he starts his speech.
"No!" An angry roar from the audience.
"Unity!" some listeners holler.
"I know what you think. I know your concerns." Stegner raises his hand in an imploring gesture. "Yes, I know that we leaders, too, make mistakes." Stegner lets his eyes wander across the ten Supervisors in the center of the hall, whose graying and thinning hair makes them stick out in the crowd. After closing his eyes for a moment, Stegner continues. "Yes, I have to confess that we weren't immune to temptation. The desire to be special had polluted our thinking. As ashamed as I might be, it cannot be denied: We have succumbed to greed." Now, Stegner lets his intensive piercing look wander across the auditorium. "Don't allow yourselves to be fooled. I'm telling you: Don't waver. After we've vanquished the enemy from outside, we'll deal with our enemies from within. When we've forced the Colonials down on their knees, then... rest assured... we'll make those people

suffer who've only paid lip-service to 'Unity', without really feeling it in their hearts."

Enraged calls of "Unity" are heard from the audience. Stegner points his finger at the banner behind the lectern, lowers his head, and closes his eyes. "Never... do you hear me... never must we forget who we are."

"Remember," the audience murmurs in awe.

"Never must we forget what we are fighting for."

"Remember..."

"Never must we forget who our enemies are."

"Remember!" All present rise from their seats. An eruption of applause.

"I've heard what you did yesterday!" Charlotte screams into my ear. "They say you did a great job at Schlesisches Tor."

The applause dies down.

"I only did what needed to be done."

"You have to be more careful, Brick. I don't want to lose you."

"I almost had her."

"Her? Are you talking about the suspect?"

"Yeah."

"Are you sure that the woman, you're looking for... do you really think that the woman with the scar is the one who killed Bull?"

"If it wasn't her who expedited Bull's demise, she's definitely had a part in it."

Charlotte playfully nudges me with her elbow, happily gazing at the stage. "I feel so sorry for those who don't belong to our Community."

Four men and a woman are led on stage. "Look, who we have here," Stegner greets the new arrivals. "Look, who's come here to meet us today." After the five people have lined up, an assistant appears, bearing a silver platter. Stegner takes a bow. On the platter rests an important symbol of our unity. We're treating this fragment of a sickle like a holy relic. With a spatula, Stegner scrapes a little bit of the fungus off its blade, slowly letting it trickle into a mortar. He adds a few drops of water and stirs the mixture with a pestle. "Once, you were lost. Once, you were the enemy." Stegner dips his index finger into the powder and paints a brown "U" onto the first man's forehead. "Now, you're one of us. From this moment on you are a Universal."

Some members of the audience can't contain their emotions any longer. They jump up from their seats. Calls of "Unity!" are resounding through the auditorium of Volksbühne.

I lean over to Charlotte. "I almost had her."

"You'll catch this woman, don't you worry."

"She couldn't have possibly done it all by herself... she must have..."

"If I didn't know you better, you'd make me wonder. Is this hurt pride, I'm hearing here?"

"She would have never escaped without help. No way. Absolutely impossible."

"Your report doesn't mention how the woman got away."

"The attack was over too fast. As if the Colonials had withdrawn as soon as they had what they wanted all along."

"And what were they after, you think?"

"The Colonials attacked for one reason only, which was to bail this woman out. Without the raid I would have grabbed her."

"You're groping, right?"

I grind my teeth. "I have to hunt her down."

"I'm sure you will. I have complete confidence in you. That's why I've put you on the case to begin with."

"I'll find her, I swear."

Charlotte nods her head, satisfied. "You have an idea, where to start, right?"

"Of course."

"But go to Weberwiese first. That's where yesterday's captives are currently interrogated."

"Weberwiese? Why are you torturing me? You know, I'm not into toast..."

"Just forget about your personal feelings. You and Toaster need... you will try to get along."

"Is this an order?"

"You're someone who knows his duties. Therefore, I see no reason to order you around." When Charlotte smiles at me, the shadows under her eyes seem more pronounced than usual. As hard as she might try to hide it, something is eating at her. "The Colonials are planning a big coup, that's what everyone says, Brick. This is why hunting down spies and collaborators has become more important than ever. All this traitor-scum needs to be wiped out. Are you listening to what I'm saying, Brick? We can't allow anything to drive a wedge into our Community!"

"You can count on me. Like always."

"I know." Charlotte turns away.

"Why are you saying that the Colonials are planning a big coup?"

But Charlotte doesn't hear me. She's staring at the stage instead, where the woman is the last one in line. Stegner paints the "U" onto her forehead. Now all the novices bear our symbol.

"I remember the day of my own initiation as if it were yesterday," Stegner solemnly declares. "It was the day, my life was finally filled with sense and meaning again. After many years of shiftless emptiness." Stegner gazes at his audience. "Now, I ask you to remember the day of your initiations. Remember the first day in your new lives."

"Remember!" the audience calls out as one.

"All of us are parts of this wonderful Community!" Stegner hollers. "We all belong..." Emotion makes his voice waver, forcing him to start anew. "We all belong together."

"Unity!" The people raise their fists high into the air. "Unity!" they passionately repeat. Charlotte and I also join the chanting: "Unity!"

And for a moment all doubts are wiped away.

8
Volkspark Hospital, Friedrichshain, Top-Level 2

The trees in Volkspark are bare. A layer of soot and lichen covers their knotty branches. I'm standing at the tip of the solar panel, which once supplied the hospital with electric power. A western wind pushes dark billows of smoke against its weather-beaten modules. I'm thinking of Bull. He was one of the few people I was able to talk about things, usually subject to censure. I'll miss him. The elevator needs just a few seconds to bring me to sub-level 2.

"It was about time." Dr. Drexler is waiting at the entrance to the autopsy suite. "Nobody is allowed up on the roof anymore."
"I just had to risk a peek at the city from above, you know."
"And? What was it like?" Drexler waves me off with a grin. "Did you count the clouds of smoke?"
"Maybe the sky will clear up some day, you never know."
"And maybe my patients will come back to life," Drexler scoffs.
"Your patients are dead."
"That's what *you* say..." Drexler puts a hand on my shoulder. "Max," he continues, "I've got something for you." Drexler always uses my first name, while insisting that I use his last, claiming that it befits his station. No idea what he's talking about. "Well, I've analyzed the woman's blood," Drexler begins. "Good

thinking to send me the anorak she's left behind straight away."

"And? What have you found?"

"I simply can't believe it."

"What is it? Speak up."

"There's no match with the DNA data bank."

"No match?"

"I've compared her profile repeatedly with our data bank as well as with all the profiles of Colonials we have on file. There's absolutely nothing. Nada. No match."

"What does this mean?"

"Max, as you very well know we have blood samples from most Colonials on files. After each fight the body fluids left behind undergo a thorough analysis, to help us to get an idea of who our attackers are. As we're talking, my people are busy securing blood residue at Schlesisches Tor."

"Their sickles don't spare anyone; this much is clear." I touch my arm, where yesterday's cut has stopped hurting.

"Injuries are part of a soldier's job description," is Drexler's somber reply. "Same as dead people are for a forensic pathologist. According to my estimate we have blood samples of about 99% of all Colonials here."

"So many? I would have never thought."

"But nothing from this woman. No match. There's nothing about her in the data bank."

"99%, you're saying? Which would mean in reverse conclusion that one in every hundred Colonials is not on the record."

"Of course you're right, if you want to be nit-picking. But statistics aside..."

"You're a scientist, right?"

"Just listen to me for a moment. What I'm trying to say is... why is it, I'm so excited, you think? What would be the best way to put it? Well, Max, I haven't seen a new DNA profile in many years."

"In years?"

"Right."

"What, if this woman is part of an auxiliary army and was just moved to New Berlin?"

"Aren't you listening to what I'm saying? It hasn't happened in years that the data bank didn't come up with a match. And whatever gives you the idea that here might be auxiliary troops? Do you really believe that the Colonials have fresh troops waiting to join the battle? After twenty years? Where would these soldiers come from, I'm asking you?"

"From the hinterland."

"The ominous hinterland, of course! No, no, no, it just doesn't make sense."

"What if the Colonials do have children after all? A new generation of soldiers."

"Children? How old, did you think, the woman with the scar you chased was?"

"She looked damn young. Possibly only in her early twenties."

"Nonsense. In this case she would have been born shortly before the siege. There has to be another explanation. Maybe she just looks young for her age."

"No forty-year-old woman looks like she's twenty."

"Maybe your eyesight is getting bad. Or your wishful thinking is getting larger."

"I can see your wrinkles perfectly well."

"Anyway, your seemingly ageless woman has never been in combat before. She must have pulled the strings behind the scenes."

"You think, she's a Supervisor? She'd be too young for that."

Drexler frowned. "We haven't been able to catch a member of their command yet. As you know, the Colonials only send their foot soldiers into the lines. Maybe their leaders are younger than ours. We don't even know what the Colonials call their top dogs."

"But they're still very well organized."

"Yes, they're effective and put up a good fight. Max, the arrival of the woman, now of all times, after twenty years of war, must have a meaning."

"Might they be planning a major offensive?"

"A major offensive? What gives you that idea?"

"Just talking."

"You know something, don't you?"

"There are rumors..."

"What rumors?"

"Just the usual ones, circulating in the sub-level."

Drexler gives me a skeptical look. He seems to think that I'm keeping secrets from him. "Funny, you mentioned a major offensive. I rather thought of a new... a..."

"What?"

"Never mind."

"You are in possession of the DNA profiles of 99% of the Colonials. How many data sets are in your bank all together?"

"Good question. I'd like to know the answer myself. However, I've only limited access. I'm only informed if there is a match. You need to be a supervisor to keep track of how many data sets there are."

"Wait a minute. I'm not quite sure I'm following you. How can you know then that we have blood samples of 99% of the Colonials? 99% of what total are we talking about?"

"That's our own number. 99% of us have had contact with the enemy so far."

"This means it's only a speculative figure, right?"

"Call it the fantasy needed to fill a gap."

"You must be joking."

"A person has to get his numbers somewhere."

"99% of us had contact with the enemy. And how many are we?"

"We've been through that before. You know, that I can't... Max, you know that this information is top secret. The enemy would... if the Colonials knew how many of us there are, they would..." Drexler is visibly torn. He wants to tell me the truth, but something prevents him from releasing the information. Now, he's looking over his shoulder, as if in fear that the room might be bugged. We don't have many smart doctors like him left. I once caught him studying an x-ray image; there was something wrong with it, I think. Drexler looked very worried. When he noticed me, he quickly stuffed the x-ray into a drawer. I suspect that the image was one of himself. Something

is spreading inside his body. I hope it can be treated.
"And what about Bull?" I ask. "Have you done his autopsy yet?"
"The antiques dealer from Frankfurter Tor?"
"Yes, the one."
"Don't remind me. It was a complete flop."
"Flop?"
"No idea what Toaster and his guys have scraped off the floor there, but it sure wasn't Bull."
"Not Bull? What the hell are you talking about?"
"These jokers only came up with fungus slime."
"Fungus slime? Toaster said they put Bull's remains into a body bag."
"He just wanted to make fun of you."
"I can't believe it."
"Better do."
"What an asshole."
"If you want to hear my advice: Stay away from Toaster."
"You must be joking. It won't be easy."

9

Reeducation Camp Newborn XIII, Weberwiese, Friedrichshain, Sub-Level 1

The guards who escort me to the cell block for newcomers carry night sticks ready to use in the belts of their black coats. Reeducation camps are controlled by P.I.D., Newborn XIII being their special camp. The most difficult and therapy-resistant cases are detained here, that is those Colonials who have refused every kind of treatment so far. We call these tough nuts "therapy-refractory". But we don't give up on them. As there are no children being born, we need them to compensate our losses in battle. Resources are scarce inside the cauldron. This also applies to human resources, which is why we use enemy soldiers to replenish our ranks.

Toaster hasn't shown his face yet, but he can't be far. He's always to be found in the middle of things. The fact that yesterday's captives have ended up in Newborn XIII, shows the urgency of the situation. Toaster and Charlotte give the attack at Schlesisches Tor the highest priority. The cauldron is bubbling. Rumor has it that the big bang is about to happen any moment. I think so, too. I'm just not sure where the threat might come from.

I peer through the peepholes in the doors of the interrogation cells. At cell number three I hit pay dirt as it contains the Colonial I've been looking for. It's the behemoth me and my comrades managed to subdue yesterday.

"Watch out," the Secret Police officer who guards the hall warns me, pointing at his bandaged nose. His left eye sports a beautiful shiner. "He's a sly bastard, this one."

"Don't worry." I nod. "We've already met."

The policeman opens the door, and I walk into the cell. The prisoner is chained to the interrogation table. And probably has been for a while, as an acrid stench fills the air. Urine has puddled under the inmate's chair. His head has been shorn. The police officers here seem to be quite heavy-handed, because his scalp is covered with fresh cuts. Even though his head is bowed, I notice that the prisoner's eyes are following my way to the table. They're the eyes of a hunter.

"The name's Brick," I say, taking the chair across. "Something hit me on the head, but it wasn't a brick," I continue in a conversational tone. "Since then my memory isn't what it used to be."

The man raises his head and looks into my eyes. He's heavily built, his jaw is enormous. As much as he might try to play dumb, he still can't fool me. The alert look in his eyes tells me he's a smart cookie.

"Maybe you can help me to refresh my memory," I suggest.

When the man rubs his powerful neck, the chains attaching him to the table tauten. "Well, well, well, so it wasn't a brick after all."

"Why did you people attack us yesterday?"

"Let me think..." Chains rattle, when the man lowers his arms to the table. "Boredom, I guess."

"Are you kidding me? Don't you guys know of any other diversions? No entertainment shows or something like it?"

"Entertainment shows? What's that when it's at home?"

"Hmmm... boxing fights at U-Hall Max Schmeling for example. Or a sickle combat at Unity Arena. You sit at a table, watch the show, and have a drink."

"And that's what you call entertainment?"

"Depends..."

"On what?"

"On the person sharing the table with you."

"A woman, you mean."

"Not just any woman. I'm talking about a special woman. You know, the attractive blonde with the scar on her chin."

The man is silent. But I know what's going on inside his head. His eyes move up to the ceiling. He seems to recall a memory. He knows the runaway woman.

"She must be damn valuable to you people. You even risked your lives to spring her," I say. "How did she contact you? I almost had her. She didn't have time to get help."

The man leans back on his chair. "No idea who you're talking about."

"What's your name?"

"What is it to you?"

"I'd like to know the name of the man who has the nerve to lie to me."

The man scoffs. "It took four of your kind to bring me down. Do you really think I'm scared of you?"

"You remember me?"

"Any reason why I shouldn't? *My* memory isn't shot. Unlike yours."

"What do you want me to call you?"

"It's up to you."

"What about C21?"

"C21? Why C21?"

"That's what it says on the door to your cell."

"Whatever."

"Aren't you Colonials attached to your names?"

"Colonials—the word alone is proof of your ignorance."

"How old are you?"

"None of your business."

"How much time, you think, you still have left?"

The man studies me. "You really do believe that you can break my will?"

"That's not the point."

"What is the point, then?"

"To convince you to fight for the right cause."

"Is that what you're trying to achieve with your ridiculous reeducation camps? With your childish conditioning therapy?"

"You know about the therapy?"

"First, you put us in solitary confinement, starve us, and isolate us from the rest of humanity. In the next step is double-occupancy cells, where we get a little more to eat. And have a chance to chat with our cellmate. If we're well behaved, it'll soon be a cell for three, later for four, and finally group detention with full privileges. These simple conditioning techniques are meant to win us over, until we come to fully appreciate your glorious Community."

"You're well informed, I'll give you that. You guys seem to have your spies everywhere. But we're not quite as backward. We don't live in dorms."

"What do you call yourselves again? Universals? A stupid name for a gang of shallow conformists."

I ignore his insults. It's important to keep your temper during interrogations. He's not supposed to notice the contempt I feel, for him as a person and for Colonials in general. For twenty years they have been forcing a brutal war on us. I think of the countless victims. Of the innocent people they butchered. And now this bastard has the nerve to lecture me? But I need to control my anger. I need to be relentless. Relentless and detached. "What did the woman with the scar want in the antique shop?"

The door to the cell opens. I hear the sound of a toaster popping bread. Immediately my mouth waters. Damned Pavlovian reflexes. Toaster walks into the interrogation room. "What are you doing with my prisoner?" he barks at me, distracting me for a moment. C21 grabs me by the hand and pulls me close. I feel his strength. "If Zoe wants to talk to you, she'll find you," he whispers into my ear.

10
Outpost Kreuzberg, Sub-Level 1

The tunnel behind the subway station Schlesisches Tor has been welded shut with slabs of metal. Almost seven feet of steel separate me from the enemy. I notice the place where the Colonials broke through the barricade, because only makeshift repairs have been made. The Colonials must have squeezed through the narrow gap one by one. I wonder, how the woman managed to escape me. She couldn't possibly have slipped through our defense lines. When our Cutters, Pullers, and Pushers took position in front of the subway train, the tunnel was completely blocked.

I walk out of the station and along the tracks toward Friedrichshain. After about a hundred yards I come across Drexler's forensic team. This must be the place where the woman jumped off the train. I see the signs of yesterday's fighting. One of Drexler's people recognizes me, giving me a wordless nod. The bodies have already been moved to the morgue. Now everyone is busy securing the DNA profiles of the injured soldiers, who escaped with their lives. Blood is scraped off the tracks, shreds of garments are put in forensic bags. Enemy soldiers usually just end up wounded, as Cutters try not to kill them. A living prisoner is worth more than a corpse.

If Toaster hadn't picked that moment to cramp my style, maybe I could have gotten some info out of C21. I noticed straight away that the guy was someone to be reckoned with. In spite of his coarse looks he seemed to have a keen wit. I'm sure he's a highly respected man among his people. It's important for us to know how the enemy ticks. We need to find out more about his strong and weak spots if we want to defeat him. The Colonials are not like us. They don't have hierarchies, but act as individuals, while we Universals coordinate every step. Universals and Colonials are members of different species. I gaze at the pipes running along the tunnel's ceiling. In spite of the brutal war between our peoples, there is a kind of co-operation when it comes to energy. Sabotage is something you'd better avoid, when the odds are that you might cut off your own supply instead of harming the enemy. There might be a war raging, but rules are rules.

C21 has called the woman with the scar Zoe. What, if she didn't retreat with the other Colonials? What, if she took a different escape route? A chicken ladder leads up to the ceiling, where the pipes are. In the antique shop the woman got away via the heating vent of the AC system. She seems to like the warmth. Is her name really Zoe, as C21 has claimed? A shrill alarm yanks me back into the present. The siren blares six times. A general alert. And at the wrong time, too. Drexler's men quickly pack up their stuff and head toward U-atrium RAW on foot. I'll follow later, I tell them. When they are out of view, I climb the rungs up to the heating pipe. The seal on the inspection flap has been broken. General alert or not, Zoe must not escape me again. It's a matter of professional honor to catch her.

11
Nearby Schlesisches Tor, Sub-Level 1

I don't feel like a headhunter, I feel like a maintenance man. No idea, how long I've been crawling through this heating pipe now. My flashlight died on me a few minutes ago. I can only hope that there will be neither a grill blocking my way nor a booby-trap I might trigger.

About thirty feet ahead there is a large hole in the pipe, a damage obviously caused by the explosion of an IED. It must have happened some weeks ago, as the metal is already covered with fungus lichen. I peer outside, where a bridge soars above my head. A three-winged building rises from the smoke. I must be in the dried-out bed of River Spree, somewhere around Jannowitzbrücke. The pipe hasn't led me to Colonial territory, but right to the edge of the Forbidden Zone instead.

Visibility is hardly a hundred yards. I can't even make out the TV tower at Alexanderplatz in the haze. The eternal fire at City Castle gives the smoke a golden tinge. Again, the sirens blare. Six times. If I haven't reported to my commanding officer before the third alert, I'll be marked AWOL. I have no choice but to abandon my chase and follow the call of general mobilization. I use a bandana to cover my mouth and nose, a feeble attempt to ward off the acrid smoke. At Holzmarkt I find a hidden hatch, leading down to the sub-level. It's an entrance hardly anybody uses. I hope that the iris scanner there will work. For a moment, the buildings on the Kreuzberg bank of the river appear in the clouds of smoke.

12
Flak Tower at Humboldthain, Top-Level 1

The fireballs pelt down on the enemies, glowing the metal plates of their tanks, bringing death and destruction. The four catapults on top of the flak tower relentlessly spew forth their fiery load. The enemies redouble their efforts and try to break through at Gesundbrunnen. Only about fifty yards separate their tanks from our barricades of barbed wire, which block the access to Badstrasse. We have to stand our ground. Badstrasse is the gateway to the heart of the cauldron.

Visibility is close to zero. I clear the soot off the goggles of my gas mask. The inside of the goggles is fogged by humidity. As much as I might loathe gas masks, I don't have a choice. There's too much dust in the air to breathe without protection. This section of the front has been fiercely fought over for months now. It's a tenacious struggle over a cityscape of rubble. Ruined buildings are jutting from the ground like rotten teeth. Brownish fungus lichens are the only living things that grow around here. I can make out the first tank that's aiming for our defense line. Those cobbled-together tanks have a weak spot: the scaled armor above the propulsion system. My perch on top of the flak tower gives me the perfect line of fire.

The commanding officer in the flak tower likes working with me. He knows me as a reliable fighter. As I know my weapon like the inside of my hand, I can easily calculate the flight path of my harpoon.

Again, my arrow strikes home. When pulling back the steel cable, I manage to pry a metal plate from the scaled armor, giving our marines behind the barricades a chance to hurl their Molotov cocktails into the gaping wound. When the tank's engine catches fire, the explosion blasts the protective armor into shreds. The crew tries to get away, but our Cutters are ready. The storm troopers' sickles are attached to long poles. Those Colonials still able to walk are tripped from afar. Two enemies, who are writhing on the ground, their bodies afire, are relieved of their misery. The Pullers catch the survivors with slings like stray dogs. No time to take a breath, because the next tank is already rolling up. The barricade is unsurmountable; the vehicle gets stuck. A hail of Molotov cocktails seals its fate. There's no time for the crew to get out, the men burn to death inside their colossus of steel. The advancing infantry is pelted with balls of flames. Our catapults are well oiled and firing away. There's nothing left for me to do here. I watch one of our Marines climbing the barricade and waving our flag. The surviving Colonials withdraw. We have successfully driven back the enemy from this section of the front. My hit has earned me an extra ration of food. What week is this again? Blue or yellow? I think, I'll exchange the jelly for something else.

13

Residential Tower "Unity 1", Kollwitzplatz, Prenzlauer Berg, Top-Level 2

"Didn't I tell you?" Charlotte looks at me, a triumphant grin on her face. "Didn't I tell you there was trouble in the air?"

"Yes, you did." I dust off my coat, feeling intensively out of place in this posh residential facility for Supervisors. Ornaments on the walls, red carpets, neon lights with textile lampshades. The luxurious illusion of safety. I, however, won't be fooled. The episode at the flak tower has once again shown me the true face of the city we live in.

"The offensive was overdue," Charlotte says. "Pent up tension needed a valve."

"Yeah." I nod. "Like with an earthquake. It builds up and up, and eventually the ground starts to shake."

"Just that it's different this time, Brick. Badstrasse, Frankfurter Allee, Landsberger Allee, the Colonials have attacked along a wide front. Rings a bell, doesn't it?"

"Three points of attack. You're thinking of the spring offensive five years ago, aren't you?"

"Exactly."

"Is it actually spring right now?"

"What difference does it make?"

"Maybe, we'll catch a bit of sunlight."

"You know very well that this is never going to happen, Brick. The only thing that definitely *will* happen is the major offensive the Colonials are going to launch against us rather sooner than later. We need to be especially careful now. This first attack was clearly a test-balloon to check out our defenses."

"Maybe, the sun will show its face after all."

Charlotte smiles at me. "I envy you for your optimism."

I point at the door of the apartment, where we have arranged to meet. "My optimism is probably not the reason you made me come here today."

"No." Charlotte breaks the P.I.D. seal on the door. "Ludger Neumann, 61, Supervisor and member of the inner circle of command."

When I enter the place, I can't suppress an appreciative whistle. "High brass, for a change."

"Stop fooling around," Charlotte scolds me. But my lack of respect doesn't really seem to annoy her. She rather looks amused. A quick smile moves across her face. Charlotte's obviously no friend of Ludger Neuman. I notice a dark stain on the rug. The man must have been standing in front of his picture window, when he died. "No matter if Supervisor or humble marine, we're all the same in death," I observe.

"The P.I.D. has collected the evidence and carted the corpse to the forensic pathology department."

I see bullet holes in the rug. The murderer used a firearm. Neumann was sent to the great beyond, while prone on the floor. The projectiles must have gone straight through his body. What kind of special ammo has this much penetrating power?

Charlotte's eyes have followed mine. "Executed with three rounds. Like the vic at Frankfurter Tor."

"There's a connection between the two murders, you think?"

"I'm convinced there is."

"A serial killer?"

"It wouldn't be the first one in New Berlin."

"Right..." I nod. My memory might not be the best but I still remember the last serial murders. "The Crazy Killer of Charlottenburg."

"The case still hasn't been solved. When the Colonials took over West City, investigations came to an end."

"The Crazy Killer was an enormously strong man." I stare out of the picture window. Top-level 2, 160 feet above New Berlin. Visibility is less than fifty feet. Billowing smoke always looks the same, no matter how high up you are. This much is sure. "But the MO differs. The Crazy Killer committed his murders with his bare hands. The Speedy Killer uses a gun."

"Speedy Killer?"

"Toaster thinks Bull was a Speedy."

"What's that supposed to mean? Speedy, like fast-forward putrefaction? Do you really believe these urban myths? Nonsense. Toaster must have been joking."

"I believe what I see. There was nothing left of Bull. And looking at this gooey muck on the rug here, it seems to be the same story with Neuman."

"I've already told you that Neuman's body was transported to the forensic pathology department. Just like Bull's."

"According to Dr. Drexler, all what was left of Bull was fungus slime."

"Dr. Drexler? He shouldn't be doing any more... has Drexler actually performed the autopsy? You know, the man has a shady reputation."

"Drexler is a good doc."

Charlotte scoffs. "I'll arrange for a *real* pathologist to do Ludger's autopsy."

"You don't trust my judgement?" I study the grill covering the AC shaft. The seal hasn't been broken. No one has entered the apartment via the heating system.

Charlotte gives me a challenging stare. I know that only some of her derogatory comments are aimed at Drexler. She's thinking about putting another headhunter on the case. "I don't understand why you're fixed on the woman with the scar so much," Charlotte says. "She must have been just a thief, breaking into the antique shop at the wrong time."

Even though I don't believe in coincidence, I choose not to contradict Charlotte and remain silent. I've overstepped the mark already. She has the power to take away my authorization anytime. If she felt that I constituted a threat to the community, she'd take me off the case. Friendship or not.

14

Café "Spreeblick" on the Gallery, Shopping Mall in U-Atrium Helmholtzplatz, Prenzlauer Berg, Sub-Level 1

"How can you eat this stuff voluntarily?" Drexler eyes me with revulsion. "I have a hard time to even get down my daily rations."

"That's because you're a frugal person." I spoon the rest of the jelly off my plate. "The yellow jelly tastes better than usual, I think."

Drexler is absent-minded and irritated. "The same slop for twenty years. The guy who was in charge of food supplies ought to be shot."

"As long as it isn't toast..."

"Sometimes I suspect that it's this jelly why there aren't any children being born. Maybe they put something in it."

"What might that be?"

"I'd love to check our rations for added hormones, but we don't have the facilities in our lab any longer. Everything's going downhill, Max. We only have two functioning CTs left at the hospital, can you imagine? In the beginning we had fifteen. We have to salvage the broken ones for spare parts."

"If we had all the resources we needed, we wouldn't be stuck in the cauldron. But the sad fact is that we're even having trouble to hold our position."

Drexler looks around sullenly. "Why do we meet here of all places? Café Spreeblick, what a stupid name. You can neither see River Spree, nor can you get coffee."

"But there are other attractions instead," I protest. The waitress appears to clear our table. When I smile at Felicitas, she smiles back before she walks away.

Drexler frowns. "We're meeting here because of *her*? Really? You're nuts, that's what you are!"

"Bullshit. I just wanted to discuss the case with you in private."

"You didn't mention her before when we talked on the intercom."

"Felicitas is a genuine sweetie. No idea where she has been hiding all this time. A woman like her wouldn't have escaped my notice, believe me."

"Max, you know me as a true-blue Universal. But I'll never be a friend of this free love thing going on in New Berlin."

"Don't be so hard on me. It's war-times." I snap my fingers. "Any moment everything can be over."

"There have been too many women popping up from nowhere recently."

"What are you trying to say?"

"The woman with the scar. And now this one... what's her name? Felicitas?"

"What are you getting at? That Felicitas might be a Colonial spy?"

"I don't know what to think. That's exactly the problem."

"Everybody's starting to go crazy. Charlotte is talking about an imminent major attack all the time."

Drexler nods. "The cauldron's boiling."

"Anyway, we're not very well prepared for such an event. The gaps in our lines in the trenches and at the flak tower are hard to miss. We're running out of fighters."

"They'll mobilize all of us, if it comes to that. Maybe they'll even put me in a uniform."

"You?"

"I've been officially suspended from office."

"Really? Shit!"

"Dr. Todt has performed Neuman's autopsy."

"Your colleague at the department? Todt almost sounds like *Tod*, death, a great name for a forensic pathologist."

"Todt's a brown-noser, if you've ever seen one. When he writes his report, it'll say just what the P.I.D. wants to read."

I study Drexler. He is short of breath and pale. I feel guilty. I shouldn't have mentioned his name in my conversation with Charlotte. "I'm sorry, you..."

"Don't worry," Drexler interrupts. "It's not the first time I've been suspended."

"No other pathologist's fit to hold the candle to you."

"You're not kidding me, right?"

"You know I don't like to blather."

"No, you don't." Drexler gives me a contemplating look. "I've thought about what you said the other day. Maybe your theory has something to it."

"Toaster wasn't joking, you mean?"

"I have to admit that I left something out last time. It wasn't only fungus slime I had on my autopsy table."

Now, I'm getting curious. "What else did you find?"

"I was able to extract human DNA. Bull's genetic profile, without a doubt. If it really were Bull's remains in this body bag, all his bones and organs had completely dissolved. As if the body had been dunked in acid."

"Bull was a Speedy, after all?"

Drexler is staring into space. "Why did P.I.D. take me off the case, even though Charlotte Fleming thinks we're dealing with a serial killer? In this case it would be especially important to have both bodies, or whatever is left of the victims, autopsied by the same pathologist."

"I've no idea what's going on with Charlotte. She's been putting me under a lot of pressure recently and insists, I'm on a wild goose chase. You want to know what else struck me as weird?"

"What?"

"When Charlotte talked about the murders, she used the word 'executions'."

"This business stinks to high heaven. Your boss knows more than she cares to admit. The P.I.D. must be somehow involved."

"Might there be some truth to this Speedy legend, after all? Do you know more about it? Spit it out!"

Drexler massages his temples. "Give me a little more time, Max. But one thing is clear: Every legend contains a grain of truth."

15
Club Cassiopeia, U-Atrium RAW, Sub-Level 1

"For 8,000 Credits I'm on." As the man leans back, the illumination sphere paints thousands of light dots on his face. Like most Outsiders, the man wears piercings in his nose and ears. The permanent use of Illusion has turned his teeth into brown stumps. His name is Rubio. The manager of Cassiopeia vouches for him. Cassio has arranged the contact for me. I'm still not convinced that Rubio will be able to help me. "What's it like in the Forbidden Zone?"
Rubio lights his water pipe. "Let's put it this way: If Friedrichshain is earth, Alexanderplatz is Mercury."
"Sounds cozy."
"If you don't watch out, you're barbecued like a pig."
I think that Rubio's laying it on with a trowel to raise the price. On the other hand, it's impossible to get correct information about the Forbidden Zone the official way. It's absolutely illegal to set foot there. And therefore there's no way of knowing if the rumors circulating in the sub-level are true or not. There's only one thing that can be safely assumed: Alexanderplatz is a place better to be avoided. Since the beginning of the siege, the subterranean fuel depots on Museumsinsel have been burning like the flares of an oil refinery. The fire raging in the center of New Berlin is the result of one of the first acts of sabotage the Colonials launched against us. "Cassio thinks you know your way around the Zone?" I ask.
"Yep." Rubio puffs on his water pipe. The vapor rising up into the air is flavored with essential oils. I

smell mint and eucalyptus. It's like flashbacks from a time long ago. Powerful and fleeting at once. The steam wafts up to the ceiling, where it dissolves. We need to remember. I need to remember. "Who are the people you smuggle into the Zone?"

Rubio gives me a suspicious look. "Cassio is a friend, you said?"

"I wouldn't call him exactly a friend. Our relationship is purely business."

"Business." A satisfied nod from Rubio. "I like honest answers."

"Why do people want to enter the Zone?"

"What are you talking about?"

"I'm just wondering what's so interesting about Mercury?"

Rubio stretches out on the sofa. "Many things... depends."

"Have there been any... let's say special activities recently?"

Rubio happily puffs on his water pipe, taking his time. "Your name's Brick?"

"That's what they call me."

"My world is different from yours, Brick."

"Different, how?"

"Us Outsiders aren't like you guys. Things you Ordies think are special, are routine for us. We see things, which remain hidden to you." *Ordies* is the Outsiders' word for ordinary people, that is for the rest of society. Rubio lifts his water pipe to gaze at the water inside the glass bulb from below. "Our world is upside-down," he continues. "And this being the case is the reason, you're here."

"8,000 Credits are a stiff price," I reply.

"Rubio Tours offers you an all-inclusive package. Maps, protective gear, and, last but not least, the services of your very personal guide."

"The guide being you."

"At Rubio Tours it's the boss himself behind the wheel."

"3,000 Credits as a down payment, another 5,000 in case of success."

Rubio smiles a cynical smile. "Oh, yeah! I just love it! A success-oriented meritocracy!" He salutes. "Yesssir! In the twentieth year of our valiant struggle against the armies of the devil, the glorious Universals will be victorious. Hail the fallen heroes! Hail our ever so holy Community!"

"You'd better watch your mouth."

"Or else? Are you going to throw me in a camp, too?"

"I only wanted to say that the walls have ears, even at RAW."

"As if I..." Rubio says with a hostile glare. "You know exactly, who I am. You leave me alone, because for you I'm a useful idiot. Look at him, you say. Look what happens to those who leave our Community. What a freak! Do you want to end up like this twitching wreck? His bad teeth, yikes! His dirty clothes, his..."

"Enough! You'll get your money, if I make it back alive."

Rubio's posture relaxes visibly. He leans forward, extending his hand. "Deal."

I shake it. Maybe Rubio is smarter than I first thought. But something bothers me about him. It's not that he's peddling Illusion. That's to be expected from an Outsider. Hell. Even the most exemplary Universal is not immune to vices. The thing I don't like about Rubio is that he samples his own merchandise, which makes him unpredictable. But I have no choice. I need to get into the Forbidden Zone, if I want to track down Zoe.

16

P.I.D. Headquarters, U-Atrium Rosenthaler Platz, Mitte, Sub-Level 1

"Identifying P.I.D. special agent Max Hofstetter, service number 45634, clearance level B1..."

The central computer has a female voice. I like it and sometimes I even imagine that it's trying to flirt with me. At least it does when I talk to it as if it were a woman of flesh and blood. I remember the time I asked Drexler if it's possible to trigger any desire in AI. Drexler just raised his brows, never deigning me an answer. Our time on earth is limited, that's his standing phrase in cases like this. I kind of like the idea that something permanent will remain of my many conversations with the computer. A bit of intimacy, or whatever you want to call it. Fact is that I'm not immune to certain fantasies raising their heads, when a woman's voice whispers the answers to me I need for my research. I'm a hunter, after all. Not only when I'm paid. I'm thinking of Drexler's derogatory remarks about the polyamorous lifestyle popular in New Berlin. He tends to switch off the speech function of his computer. Sometimes I wonder what drives him professionally. What's his incentive?

"Special agent Max Hofstetter, how can I help you?" The intercom's iris scanner switches off after verifying my identity.

"How can anyone ignore a sensuous voice like this?" I ask, still lost in thought.

"Please state a precise question, Sir."

"Weren't we on first-name basis already?"

"The address is to be kept short and formal. Users are to refrain from pleasantries and frivolous comments. Keep in mind that the terminal will only be available for ten minutes, starting now."

"Sounds like fun."

"You have nine minutes and thirty seconds left."

"Why has my access been restricted?"

"Access has been restricted since the commencement of the National Emergency Act."

Charlotte hasn't exaggerated. There's something going on. The last time the National Emergency Act was put into place was five years ago when we lost West City to the Colonials. I need to hurry. If martial law will be declared, I won't report to the P.I.D. anymore, but to the army. "Are forensic requests permitted?"

"Yes, such requests are processed here."

"Please conduct a comparative evaluation of the projectiles used in the murders of Paul Bull and Ludger Neuman."

"The cases Paul Bull and Ludger Norman haven't been classified as murders but as unnatural deaths."

"Unnatural deaths?"

"This is how it is stated in the files."

"Who stated it?"

"You are not authorized to receive this information. The information is subject to clearance level A4."

"One more question: Did the cartridges found next to Paul Bull's body come from the same weapon than the one found in Ludger Neuman's apartment?"

"Correct."

"What's the registration number of the gun?"

"The registration number is not stated."

"How come? Negligence?"

"I do not possess information in regard to the reasons for missing entries."

"What type of gun is it?"

"It is a XT305."

This gun comes with a muffler. It is used by special forces. The XT305 has been taken out of commission many years ago, because there was no more ammo to be had. "How many weapons of this type are listed in your register?"

"Fifty-six weapons."

"Who are the owners?"

"The weapons are centrally stored in the gun room inside P.I.D. headquarters."

"Here, you mean?"

"Please state a precise question."

"You were saying that all XT305s are in the possession of P.I.D.?"

"Correct."

I rub my parched lips. Someone in P.I.D. is involved in the serial killings. That much is clear. Charlotte doesn't trust her own people. She's letting investigations simmer on a low flame. The detective squad will only take action after the incidents at Frankfurter Tor and Kollwitzplatz are classified as murders. And as long as this isn't the case, there's only one option open to Charlotte. She's playing with fire. "Which headhunter is currently on the case?"

"Max Hofstetter, service number 45634."

"Good man..."

"… and Tom Schächter, service number 34673."
Bingo. I knew it. Charlotte has put a second headhunter on the case."

"You have another five minutes left. Please tell me if you want to terminate the session prematurely."

"Just a moment..." Tom is a rogue loner and absolutely loyal to Charlotte. He and I have had a serious altercation once. Another controversy won't lead to anything good. I need to know who's been at and around the crime scenes. "Please give me access to the footage of the surveillance cameras in front of the antique shop 'Before Our Times' and inside the elevators of the residential tower 'Unity One.' Download the footage of last week."

"This is not possible. Clearance level A4 is required."

I bang on the terminal in frustration. How am I to do my job, if I'm obstructed at every turn? Why is Charlotte doing this to me? Hell, what is she up to?

17
Forbidden Zone, Alexanderplatz, Ground Level

The TV tower is an imperial presence, soaring from the rubble with the blazing flames on Museumsinsel as a background. My throat tightens. "Give me my protective gear. Hurry!"

"Protective gear?" An amused look from Rubio. "Think you need one?"

"Are you joking? What am I paying you for?"

"Questions, always questions. The Observators in U-Atrium Weinmeisterstrasse needed to be bribed. And I have to give a little something to the Diggers who keep the tunnel clear for me. Rubio Tours is a complex business machinery."

"Oiled with my Credits."

"Do you think it was our pretty faces that got us past the checkpoints?"

"You should have told me how it works."

"Are you worried they might get us?"

"I would have thought that you had some more refined tricks in store. Bribery? What a steamroller approach. Now, we're at the mercy of those Observators."

"You worry too much. If the Observators give us away, you can always claim you didn't know we were going into the Forbidden Zone. Just tell them, this dirty Outsider has tricked you."

"Have you ever been interrogated by the P.I.D.? Do you have any idea what they do to people to make them talk?"

"Stay cool, man. You really do have a stick up your butt." Rubio offers me a vial of Illusion."

I refuse. "The fumes at Alexanderplatz are extremely toxic. We'll choke to death here."

"You're so naïve, man. That's just Universal propaganda. The air here isn't any worse than it is at Boxhagener Platz on your side." Rubio takes a deep breath, coughs, and spits on the ground. "That's the proverbial cosmopolitan air of Berlin, right?"

I have to watch where I'm going. A crater yawns ahead. U-Atrium Alexanderplatz is no more. When the fuel depots on Museumsinsel went up in flames, it must have caused a shock wave. The U-Atrium's cupola was blasted away like the lid off a pot. Pipes are leading nowhere. Vapor rises from broken shafts. The shopping mall in the sub-level lies in ruins. When Rubio slaps my shoulder, I fear for a second that he's trying to shove me into the abyss. He finds my worried reaction hilarious. "Welcome to the Zone. Well, I like it here. All this beautiful destruction makes me feel right at home. Have you ever been to my crib? You need to come see me sometime."

The Urania World Clock is covered in layers of lichen, dirt, and oily sludge. The buildings at Alexanderplatz are beyond recognition under a coating of organic material and remind me of a sandcastle after a sudden downpour. "At least the fungus is happy as a fiddle here at Alex." Rubio picks up a length of steel pipe from the ground to scratch at the lichen blanketing the World Clock. The mass is hard as a rock.

Wind hits my face, the chimney-effect in this place providing a steady movement of air. The eternal flames want to be fed. "If we just had some sunshine now and then," I murmur to myself.

"You Ordies are such wimps. As soon as you set one foot outside your air-conditioned malls, you start whining."

"I need to get to Jannowitzbrücke. You understand?"

"What do you want there of all places?"

"None of your business."

"You know that there is no River Spree any longer, right? Which means that Jannowitzbrücke isn't a real bridge either. Names don't mean nothing no more."

"Rubio, my man, you're a real philosopher."

"Let's check out the scene around Alexanderplatz, right? I'll show you some attractions. At Neptunbrunnen, that's right behind the TV Tower, there's this huge crater. It's actually a little pond now. We might take a dip. That is, *you* might take a dip and I'll watch how you're doing." A nasty laugh from Rubio.

"No wonder, you Outsiders have such a lousy reputation."

"What's wrong? Where's your sense of humor?"

"I don't like being lied to."

"You're still mad because of the protective gear?"

"A deal is a deal."

"Yeah, yeah, right." Rubio pulls something from his pocket. It's a wet wipe. "Take this instead."

"Don't push it."

"You're still not happy? These thingies are extremely rare. Individually packaged and lemon-scented. They'll get your little paws squeaky-clean."

"You're a nuisance. Has anyone ever told you that?"

"I'm a victim of circumstance." Rubio scrapes his shoe across the ground.

"What is it now?"

"There has to be a hatch somewhere around here. But this annoying fungus just covers everything. The stuff's all over the place, like ivy at a cemetery. I just need to find this hatch. There are depots that haven't been looted yet. But you have to be lucky."

"What's there to find in all this rubble?"

"You need a good nose."

"What exactly are you looking for?"

"You think, I tell you all my secrets? It's not like we are friends or so."

"I never thought so. Just take me to Jannowitzbrücke. Afterwards you're free to do whatever you want."

18

Forbidden Zone, Jannowitzbrücke, Ground-Level

"Give me a hand, will you?" Rubio's trying to pick up a steel strut from the ground. A gap yawns underneath. "Maybe coming here wasn't such a bad idea, after all."

I help Rubio to get the strut out of the way. "I need to go on. To the river bed. That's where I lost her," I say.

"*Her?*" Rubio shines his flashlight into the crack. "You're looking for a woman?"

"Well, I... yes."

"And you think you'll find yourself a woman in the Forbidden Zone?"

"That's my business."

"Just look around. What are the odds, you think? There are no fair damsels to be seen anywhere."

"Very funny."

"What do you do for a living, by the way? You look like one of these salesman types who're trying to talk you into buying something you don't need."

"You're making fun of me, right?"

"Maybe I am..."

"Don't do that."

"You shouldn't worry so much about other people's opinion."

"Easy for you to say. You're an Outsider. Nobody cares what you think."

"You'd better get your screw-you factor upgraded."

"I'm a patriot and I love my country. If everybody thought like you do, society would fall apart."

"It's always the same old song. Can't you guys in Universal-Town come up with something more original?"

"The enemy is standing on the other bank of River Spree. If the Colonials win this war, it will be the end of our culture. No more Outsiders. And also no more Rubio who gives a shit about the system."

"You're beating a dead horse. And it's been dead for a very long time."

"I'm a Universal. I've sworn an oath to defend this city."

"Brick, Brick, what am I to do with you? Where did you get this funny name from anyway? Why do they call you Brick?"

"Something hit me on the head. But it wasn't a brick."

"This explains a lot, of course."

"Save your breath. You won't get a rise out of me so easily."

Rubio grins. "It was worth a try."

"You're a real weirdo, aren't you?"

"Is it true what Cassio says? That you're a headhunter? You don't look like one of those bloodhounds."

"What's a bloodhound supposed to look like?"

"No idea. The guys who show up at RAW occasionally are members of the tribe 'use your fists first, ask questions later'. Glorified rent-a-cops, if you ask me."

I think of Tom. "We also have a few tough guys among us."

"To go man hunting is a strange way to make a living."

"You didn't mind taking my Credits."

"Hey, the only way to beat the system is to fuck it."

"And how do you fend for yourself? Apart from fleecing the people you smuggle into the Forbidden Zone."

"If you light me the way, I'll show you something." After handing me the flashlight, Rubio squeezes his body through the gap. "This is a depot, I think. The looters have been here already, but..." Rubio coughs. "This damn fungus. The spores hurt my lungs."

"Are you okay?" I can't see Rubio any longer. The beam of my flashlight illuminates a row of shelves. "Rubio?"

"Hell, I can't believe it! Is it really true? These morons have actually missed something!"

"What did you find?"

"Patience, my man, patience!" Rubio squeezes back through the gap. He's holding a suitcase that is overgrown with lichen. The case is emblazoned with a red symbol. A snake writhing around a staff. The staff of Aesculapius, if I remember right. Fungus growth obscures the name underneath. I can only identify the first and the last letters. I and S. It's enough to tell me the entire name: *Icarus.*

"Brick, from now on you're my lucky charm." Rubio rubs his hands together. "Watch out." Slowly and carefully he opens the case. "I'd never have thought that I'd live to see the day. Just look!" He caresses the vials resting on a bed of foam rubber. "This is premium-quality Illusion." Rubio takes one vial out to study the label. "Lot A354-212... Samples from an A-lot! Holy smoke! And none of these darlings is damaged."

"Are you serious? You come to the Forbidden Zone to look for drugs?"

"We're all looking for something. You're looking for a woman, I'm looking for junk." Rubio tilts back his head, breaks open a vial and dribbles Illusion onto his tongue. "Oh, my God!" He takes a deep breath. "This will be the trip of the millennium!"

"Are you nuts?! Have you forgotten, where we are? I mean, just look around. You can't do this right now..." I grab Rubio and shake him. "We need to turn back!" Too late. Rubio crumples. His pupils are dilated, his body goes limp. "Rubio! What did you do? Rubio! You fucking idiot!"

19
Forbidden Zone, Jannowitzbrücke, Ground-Level

A dirt path leads from the dry bed of River Spree toward Alexanderplatz. I can clearly see the footprints, outlined in the layer of fungus. It seems to be a frequently traveled route. Has the woman with the scar used it, too? I can't make out any blood. But Zoe must be injured. My harpoon has struck her arm. The bloodstains on the anorak leave no room for doubt. Why didn't she try to reach Colonial territory? It doesn't make sense. What does she want in the Forbidden Zone?

Suddenly, I'm starting to feel uncomfortable. I turn around. Someone is watching me. I pull my harpoon gun from its holster. It can't be Rubio. When I left him he was drifting in outer space. I've pulled him under a ledge of a building, hoping that he'd have slept it off by the time I return. I worry that there might be Colonials lurking around here. But the fire on Museumsinsel should be enough to keep them away. It's impossible to access Alexanderplatz from West-City. If you try to make your way around the wall of flames, you end up on our turf.

Here in the Forbidden Zone the fungus grows thicker than it does in Friedrichshain or Prenzlauer Berg. I might not be a botanist, but even I can tell the difference. I wonder how thick the coating is that covers all the buildings. I scrape the harpoon dart of my gun across a wall a couple of times. All the while, thousands of thoughts are flashing through my head. If the symbol on the case with the legend "Icarus" really is a staff of Aesculapius, the contents of the vials must be some kind of medical emergency supply. Was Illusion originally meant to be used as medication? The Icarus-case in Bull's antique shop didn't bear a symbol, its contents, however, were even more mysterious. Zoe stole the artifact from the case. What is it used for? If you want to believe the rumors circulating in the sub-level, you need to be a Supervisor to know the real meaning of the artifacts. My harpoon dart slowly works its way through the coat of fungus, which is hard as stone. Even though the groove I've dug is almost one inch deep, it doesn't yet reach down to the wall proper. A white liquid is trickling down the tip of my arrow. I stop. It looks like the fungus is bleeding; the goo sealing the cut as if trying to heal a wound. The fungus doesn't seem to be happy with me. When I dip my finger into the sticky substance, my skin starts to tingle. I lick my finger without thinking and a sweetish taste spreads in my mouth…

I'm not alone. I knew all along that I was being watched. Someone is sitting at the bank of River Spree. The man is dozing, a fishing rod in his hand. I walk over to him. "Do they bite?" I ask him.

The man turns around. He's Paul Bull, the owner of the antique shop. He points at the dry river bed. "It needs to be filled with water." Bull lifts up his T-shirt. He has a plug where his belly button should be. When Bull pulls the plug, a fountain of water gushes out. "It will take some time until the river bed is full."

"If my memory just weren't so bad. You know, Bull, I used to have picnics here some time ago. With wine and all the works. But I can't remember who I was with. The woman was... she is..."

Bull gazes at me with a serious expression. "I want to talk to you about the artifact."

"Who killed you, Bull?"

"Some things are invisible to your eyes. Secret struggles. Enemies, who pull the strings behind the scenes. And friends, who kill each other. You need to risk a peek behind the facade to understand what's happening around you."

"But... but how am I supposed to do this?"

"You know the name that's the key to the truth."

"Yes, I know." I nod. "Icarus."

"Follow the path of the *Icarus*. Find the lost artifacts. Fulfill your destiny."

"Artifacts? Plural, you mean? What are the artifacts good for?"

"I can't walk a path that's meant for you."

"Where do I start searching?"

"Go down into the depths. Venture in the realm of no return."

"Can we be saved?"

Someone touches my shoulder. I turn around. Behind me there's a woman wearing an anorak. She has a scar on her chin. Zoe smiles at me. I notice the smoothness of her skin.

"Why are you still so young?"

"I'm not young."

"But you look young. Much younger than everyone else I know."

"I'm an old soul in a young body."

"Where can I... where do I find you?"

"You need to stop chasing me."

"But I'm a headhunter."

"You will only escape the darkness if you take a leap of faith."

I hear a hissing sound. Bull is gone, only his depleted shell is left on the ground. The river bed is filled with water. A starry sky above me, I'm standing on the bank of River Spree. Two moons are shining. Zoe takes my hand. An electric jolt curses through my body. It's my end, I feel it. And at the same time, I'm reborn.

20
Forbidden Zone, Jannowitzbrücke, Ground-Level

"Welcome back." Rubio is hovering over me.
I'm on the ground. "Where's the dictating machine? Will my hands still be able to hold it? Am I a material body, can I reach out and move?"
"Man, that must have been a hell of a trip."
I'm still drowsy. "What?"
"You're lucky you're still alive."
"That I'm still alive?"
Rubio sits next to me, crossing his legs. "You're back. Not many people have sampled the fungus and lived to tell the tale."
"Fungus? Sampled?"
"I really envy you. Your experience on the other side must have been the absolute bomb!"
I massage my forehead. My skull is throbbing. "Oh, God, my head hurts like hell."
Rubio offers me a bottle. It contains a clear liquid that looks like water. I hesitate.
"What's wrong?" Rubio asks. "You think I put Illusion in there?"
"Well, have you?"
"No, I've just scooped it out of the pond back there." Rubio laughs. "I think I saw a dead horse in the water. It might also have been a giant mutant frog. Who knows?"
"I'm really not in the mood for your jokes right now."
Rubio makes me drink a few mouthfuls of water. "That's two-thousand Credits."
"What?"

Rubio waves me off. "A joke, just a joke."
I realize that something is wrong. "Why am I not wearing anything? What is this thing I'm covered with, my jacket?"
"Your underwear is in the mud back there. No idea, if you want to put it on again. Your shoes are next to the pond. If you happen to come across your pants and shirt, just let me know."
"I've no idea what happened."
"Why does it worry you?"
"Because I like to be in control."
"Well, you seem to have somehow failed in this respect."
"Bull and Zoe were at the riverbank. There were two moons in the sky. Something hit me. Then, everything went blank. The absolute blackout."
"When I found you, you were hopping around buck-naked, yelling something at the top of your voice."
"I did *what?*"
"You're free at last, brother. You've rid yourself of everything that's been holding you down. I envy you so much. Sadly, my trip was a wash-out. Illusion doesn't seem to work for me anymore."
"What exactly did I yell?"
"You danced around like a madman, screaming 'Icarus! Icarus!'"
"Icarus..."
"Pretty adventurous of you to scarf down psychedelic fungus. I keep my fingers off this stuff."
"Illusion is weaker?"

"Illusion? Are you joking? Illusion is baby stuff compared to the junk you guzzled. Just think of milk versus vodka."

"I just... I only licked my finger."

"Please no erotic details of your tryst with our slimy friend. I'm already green with envy, as it is. The fungus seems to like you, or else you wouldn't be one of the chosen who have survived a tête-à-tête with Mr. Mold. I underestimated you, Brick. I have to give you that. That's not at all what I would have expected from a dyed-in-the-wool Universal. You really surprised me. Jumping around in your birthday suit. But I guess even real squares have to let it fly sometimes."

"I've no idea what hit me."

"You let go of your inhibitions, brother. You set free all your repressed sides. You must be an Outsider at heart."

"You know, Rubio, the Forbidden Zone is totally different from what I thought it would be. I should have come here much earlier. It's not that I'm an ignoramus. I often stand on Oberbaumbrücke, looking over to the Zone. But I would have never guessed... never in my life I would have thought that it is so... I don't know how to put it."

"So it really was your very first visit to the Zone?"

"Yes."

"Why did you never come here before?"

"It's against the rules."

Rubio's comment is a wry laugh. "Of course, I forgot: the RULES."

"Are you a Digger, Rubio?"

"Hell, no. Do I look as if I had a suicide wish? I go down to sub-level 5 max. Never any deeper."

"How deep are we talking about?"

Rubio looks me into the eyes. "I don't know if there's anyone who knows."

"I need to go deep down, Rubio. Deeper than anybody has before me."

21

Universal Territory, Space Catapult Skystormer VI, Hackesche Höfe, Top-Level 1

"Where have you been all this time?" Charlotte gives me the evil eye. "I've had them look for you all over the place. It was like you had vanished into thin air."

"I was out hunting." My excuse is doomed to fail. This much I know. Charlotte has brought reinforcements. I see Tom next to her. Tom is my height but has a torso much too short for his long legs. They aren't his real ones and the prostheses make his body look strangely out of proportion.

"What are you wearing?" Charlotte has noticed the grey coverall of a garbage collector under my jacket. I can't possibly tell her about my visit to the Forbidden Zone and I pray that the Observators Rubio bribed will keep their mouths shut.

I raise my eyebrows. "A minor accident in the garbage chute."

Charlotte studies me, suspicion in her eyes. "I sent a general alert to all intercoms. You haven't responded."

"I'm sorry, I wasn't at the intercom for a while. I came as soon as I saw your message."

Tom shakes his head. "I don't know if Brick's still fit to work as a headhunter, Charlotte. He's been slipping recently and doesn't focus on the job."

Tom has always been jealous of my special relationship with Charlotte. He resents me being her number one headhunter. And now he seems to think that his moment has come. I know why Charlotte has summoned both me and Tom to this place today. To the most southwestern tip of our territory, wedged in between the Forbidden Zone and Colonial turf. Him or me. Tom or I. Only one of us will survive.

A man is led into the hangar. The henchmen have pulled a bag over his head. In the old days the catapult was used for the acceleration of space shuttles. But there haven't been any shuttles for years. Meanwhile, the facility is put to quite a different use. Charlotte adjusts the orthopedic corset that supports her torso. "Tom is on the case as well now."
I won't be able to gain any brownie-points here and now. But at least I want to walk out of this hangar with my head raised. "I had problems when I tried to research something at the P.I.D. terminal. Clearance levels had been changed. Do you know who's authorized it? For my research, I definitely need..."
Charlotte silences me by raising her hand. "Look at Tom. He doesn't ask questions, but delivers answers. He has found out that the murder weapon comes from the stores of P.I.D."
"Why were the murders classified as unnatural deaths? If you..."
"Brick, Brick..." Tom interrupts me. "The killer must be P.I.D., my friend. It's an inside-job. This is why we need to be discreet. Don't you get it? Maybe the brick caused more damage than we all would like to believe." Tom makes moon eyes at Charlotte like a well-trained puppy expecting a treat.
"Enough! I don't want to hear anymore of it." Charlotte's expression is thunderous. "From neither

one of you. And no backtalk either. It's crucial for us to concentrate our efforts. Did you hear me? The enemy is in our midst. Someone is doing all they can do to destroy our community. I won't allow treason to corrode us from within." Charlotte presses the talk-button of her microphone. "Ex-Universal Jack Schneider, you have betrayed details about our defense tactics to the Colonials. The punishment for high treason is ejection from our community."

Two henchmen escort the delinquent to the catapult. I can see him balk for a moment. But he has no chance to escape the inevitable. The henchmen let him thrash about for a while, before tying him to the slide with routine movements. The executioner himself stays in the back. He has the option to intervene with his club any time, but the audience wouldn't appreciate it. Jack Schneider shall remain fully conscious until the very end.

"The sentence will be enforced immediately." Charlotte presses the launch-button. The computer starts its countdown. Tom's watching the delinquent, a sneer on his face. "This bastard traitor will finally get what he deserves. The guy's nothing but pond-scum, a waste of space. I'd give anything for the chance to tear his pathetic body into bits with my bare hands."

Charlotte raises his hand to silence him. "We don't want to desecrate this solemn moment of self-purification with words. Let us now renew our bond." Charlotte takes Tom's hand and motions him to take mine in turn. But he refuses. "What's wrong?" she asks.

"I think, Brick is... he isn't..."

Charlotte nudges him in the side. "Brick is one of us. Until he chooses differently."

Tom reaches for my hand; I feel his reluctance. Then he clamps his fingers around mine in a vise-grip. I match him and we continue compressing each other's hands until our fingertips turn blue.

"... six, five, four, three, two, one, take-off frequency initiated." The female computer voice has finished the countdown. Her inflection is always matter-of-fact, research requests at the P.I.D. terminal or executions, it doesn't make a difference to her. That's the beauty about it. The rest is silence. The slide zooms along the catapult, ejecting Jack Schneider's body from our community. It will hit ground somewhere deep in Colonial territory.

22

Reeducation Camp Newborn XIII, Weberwiese, Friedrichshain, Sub-Level 1

"Are you crazy, or what?" I wrap my bandana around the cut on my hand.

Toaster watches the blood dripping off the blade of his knife. "Sorry. Didn't see you coming around the corner." Something is wrong with Toaster. Even though his facial prosthesis has become dislodged, he doesn't try to readjust it. His wig is askew, and he doesn't seem to care about that either.

I press my finger on the wound to stop the bleeding. "Better watch out next time."

Toaster's staring at the blood trickling off his blade like a man possessed. "You're bleeding just like I do."

"Have you totally lost it now? What are you talking about?"

"Your blood isn't too viscous and has exactly the right color. Exactly what it's supposed to look like."

"What, are you nuts?"

"You're clean, I'd say." Toaster sounds disappointed.

I have no explanation for his behavior. "Why did you want to see me?"

"Everybody one by one."

"What?"

"I want to show you something. It'll be everybody's turn eventually."

"I don't have the faintest idea what you're talking about."

When Toaster looks at me, there's contempt in his eyes. He wipes the knife on his coat and sheathes it. "I was hoping you'd fail the test. I was really looking forward to it. Alas, life isn't a request concert."

I need to play for time until I understand what's going on here. "What is it you wanted to show me?"

"Follow me." Toaster leads me to an interrogation cell. The legend on the door says C21. "You've already had the pleasure..." Toaster pushes open the door. On the floor behind the table I see the prisoner's coveralls. The material is soaked in blood. I also notice shreds of skin, bones and tissue on the tiles. When Toaster picks up the coveralls, it drips slime on the floor. "There's not much left over of these thingies."

"*Thingies?*"

"Another Speedy, what do you say?"

"Where's the body? Already at the forensic pathology department?" My eyes wander over to the drain. A lot of blood went down there. I see something glinting under the grill.

"I should have known. You're just too dense to get it." Toaster gives me a condescending smile that raises only one corner of his mouth. The lack of symmetry in his face never ceases to disconcert me. "In the old days we had a Speedy once in a blue moon. But now? Now I'm having trouble to keep up with the numbers. We're being contaminated, without even realizing it."

"How did the interrogation get out of control like this?"

"Interrogation?"

"Which one of your guys has killed him?"

"My men didn't have anything to do with it. I vouch for them. The bastard managed to sneak this thing into the cell somehow." Toaster points at a sling of wire, wrapped around a table leg. "It seems that this asshole giant didn't love life all that much. And a good thing, too. This way he saved us a lot of work."

I don't believe a word Toaster's saying. C21 never took his own life. I know how it must have happened. No matter if friend or foe, nobody deserves to have Toaster torture him to death. I'm sorry for C21 and his miserable end. But I need to get a grip on myself. It's dangerous to show weakness in front of Toaster. "A prisoner committed suicide. It won't make Charlotte happy to hear that. It doesn't reflect favorably on your camp."

"Who cares? It's one dirty Colonial less."

"Has Tom come by already?"

"Why do you want to know?"

"You sound exactly like him."

"I'll run the same test with this clown on stilts, just wait and see." Toaster moves his index finger across the crack in his face as if wanting to make sure which half of it is fake. After readjusting his facial prosthesis, he straightens his wig. "Don't you worry, everyone else will get the same warm welcome you did." On his way to the door Toaster starts to sway. He seems to be dizzy and barely manages to steady himself against the wall. Time has left its mark on him. It's becoming increasingly hard for him to defend his position as an Alpha, which is based on physical strength. Toaster's living on past glory. The rival who will eventually depose of him won't give a second thought to the fact that Toaster is a living legend. "The best have fallen." Toaster repeatedly bangs his head against the wall. "All my men... my very best comrades... and what about me? I'm only surrounded by scum."

In the moment Toaster has his back to me I make use of the opportunity to lift the grid off the gutter and retrieve the shiny metal object underneath. Just in time, because Toaster turns around. "Get lost, before I change my mind," he dismisses me. And I know it isn't meant as an empty threat.

23

Volkspark Hospital, Friedrichshain, Defunct Wing, Sub-Level 3

"CT305." Drexler studies the cartridge case through his trinocular microscope. "What kind of gun is it from?"

I look at the freeze-frame on the monitor. In forty-x magnification every little scratch on the cartridge case is visible. "The P.I.D. used this type of gun for special operations. These slugs have a lot of penetrating power."

"Where did you find it?" Drexler asks.

"In a drain."

"And where exactly?"

"You don't want to know."

Drexler gives me a quick look. He seems to be paler than usual. "I had no idea that this special ammo was still around."

"What does this tell us about the killer?"

Drexler shakes his head. "Oh, boy, we're in it up to our necks."

"Amen to that." I cast a look around the depot. Since he's been suspended, Drexler's denied access to the forensic pathology department. Never being known for his lack of resourcefulness, he's just taken over some rooms in a defunct wing of the hospital. Drexler has salvaged the decommissioned appliances on the tables from all over the building. Nobody bothers him down here, but he's also completely isolated. "Does anyone know what you're doing here?"

Drexler smiles. "Todt hasn't paid me a visit so far."

"I still don't understand, how someone whose name sounds like '*Tod*'—death can work as a pathologist."

"You've said that before."

"And why doesn't Todt ever come down here?"

"He's scared."

"Scared of what?"

"The dark corridors."

"You don't happen to have sabotaged the lighting system?"

"I didn't miss my calling as a janitor, this much I admit."

"A pathologist who's scared of the dark. Why am I not surprised?"

"What happened to your hand, by the way?"

"I had a little mishap with a toaster, if you know what I mean."

"Well, well..." Drexler starts to fidget on his chair.

I put a calming hand on his shoulder. No idea what's making him so nervous. "The cartridge. What characteristics did you identify?"

"You must be joking. What do you expect from me? I'm a pathologist, not an expert for forensic firearms analysis. I don't even know what to look for."

"I can't have the cartridge checked by the P.I.D. lab. For obvious reasons." I give Drexler an encouraging pat on the shoulder. "You're a smart guy. You're setting your own standards."

Drexler's not given to vanity, but my praise still pleases him. "Well, I can give it a try. Hearts or cartridges, there can't be all that much of a difference." Drexler is moving the cartridge case around under the lens of the trinocular, until he has created a freeze-frame of the percussion cap. "The imprint of the... what do you call it, firing pin? A bit off the center, right under the digit three of the code. See, what I'm talking about? The imprint isn't round, other than it would be expected. Was the gun used a lot?"

"No idea."

"Looks like a half-moon, if you ask me."

I study the imprint of the firing pin displayed on the monitor.

"Looks like a C to me."

"C like Colonials. Might it be a secret..." Suddenly, Drexler's eyes turn inward. He slumps.

"Are you okay?" I slap his cheeks.

"Is anything wrong?" Drexler comes to again, taking a moment to get his bearings.

"You just were out for a moment. What happened?"

A tortured laugh from Drexler. "Too much work."

"Bullshit. You've been suspended." I feel that there must be more behind his fainting fit. "What's really wrong with you?"

"Oh, it's nothing."

"Has it anything to do with the x-ray image you were looking at the other day?"

"It seems to be impossible to keep a secret from you."

"Is it bad?"

Gingerly, Drexler touches his calf. He seems to be in pain. "Lung cancer. Final stage."

"Lung cancer? How did it... how did you of all people come down with lung cancer?"

"It's the air of New Berlin. The worst degree of pollution imaginable. A lethal mix of nitric oxides and free radicals."

"I still don't understand. You never go outside. You're practically always indoors, at the hospital."

"Do you think the air in the sub-level is any better than outside? The air filters aren't changed on a regular basis anymore. Which means that the indoor particle load in the air is going up and up. There're shortages wherever you look."

"Why did you never say anything?"

"Life has to go on. As long as it lasts."

"Maybe I can get you the medication you need via the P.I.D., if the hospital doesn't have any. I'm sure they've got extra supplies on store. If there're still ammo for a CT305, there also has to be a stash of meds."

"Forget it. I'm beyond treatment." Drexler clutches his calf again.

"What's this with your calf? The cancer's in your lungs, right?"

"Do you really want to see it?"

"Yes."

"Okay. But please don't start puking all over the place." Drexler rolls up his trouser leg. His calf is bandaged. When he removes the dressing, the wound oozes brown slime. I start gagging and almost lose my lunch. "This wound... oh, my God... what is this? Is there something *growing* in there?"

"It's the fungus."

"Fungus? Why don't you just clean out the wound? Hell, you're going to lose your leg."

"You don't understand, Max." Drexler takes a pill bottle from the pocket of his lab coat. *Hyposporin forte,* the label says. "I'm even taken this stuff to suppress my immune system."

"What are you talking about. You mean, you're suppressing your immune system on purpose for the inflammation... for the inflammation to spread? Are you serious?"

"I'll try to explain. When I took antibiotics, it reduced the fungus infestation in the wound. I was relieved. Then, however, I took a look at my x-ray and noticed that my tumor had grown instead. Grown a lot. Within a short period of time."

"Do you mean to say that the fungus blocks the growth of the tumor?"

"There's a direct correlation between fungus growth and tumor growth. Without this infection, the tumor would have killed me by now, I swear."

"But the fungus? You'll lose your leg?"

"Better my leg, than my life." Drexler produces a second pill bottle. It's an antibiotic. He's weighing the bottles with immunosuppressor and antibiotic in both hands. "How would you decide, Max?"

24
Club Cassiopeia, U-Atrium, RAW, Sub-Level 1

"The woman you're looking for is called Zoe?" Rubio's sitting in front of Club Cassiopeia. He claims to be birdwatching. As if there were any birds inside U-Atrium RAW. There isn't even a chirp coming from the speakers.

I like Rubio's sense of humor.

"Yeah, Zoe," I say.

"Why haven't you told me before?"

"I first wanted to get to know you better."

"And now you know me?"

"I know you as well as a headhunter can know an Outsider."

Rubio smiles. "I've seen your Zoe around a few times. The first time was maybe a month ago. She always hung with the Diggers."

"With the Diggers? Why?"

"Brother, you're the one who nibbled on the fungus. That's why you're enlightened. I'm just a lowly Illusion junkie."

"What's the Diggers' names?"

"Phil and his people. This Phil, he's a real crazy type. Needs four vials of Illusion to get a kick. I haven't seen him and his guys for a while around RAW."

Someone pushes open the door to the club. It's Cassio. "What are you guys doing out here?"

I don't want Cassio to know that I'm in RAW to investigate. "Even headhunters need a little something now and then." I open my mouth, pretending to dribble Illusion on my tongue.

Cassio smiles. "My girls are waiting upstairs. Blonde and squeaky clean. You've enough Credits on you, I hope?"

Rubio remains silent, until Cassio has vanished inside his club. "I don't trust the man. He wears an inked U on his forehead. This shows me how he ticks. He'd shop us anytime, given the chance."

"You want me to put Cassio under pressure a bit? I could sic P.I.D. on him. I know someone, who's been looking for reasons to crack down on RAW for a while."

Rubio waves me off. "Leave it. I'm not informing on anyone."

"I wouldn't have thought that of you..." My alarm bells ring. I look around the U-Atrium. There's something wrong. I don't like the quiet in here. Not at all. Normally, the RAW is a hot spot of trouble. There's always someone arguing or fighting.

Rubio, too, seems to sense danger. "Shit," he whispers. "We need to split. Now."

The attackers storm the U-Atrium without a warning, entering the domed hall from all sides. We're trapped. Our people frantically run around in circles like a flock of startled sheep. But there's no way out. The Colonials have already blocked the exits.

For a moment, everything comes to a standstill. The Colonials outnumber us, and that's not our only problem. Some of us are high on drugs, others stagger from lack of sleep. Nobody is ready to put up a fight. Meanwhile, we've been surrounded by the enemies, who point the sickle blades of their spears at us. But instead of attacking us, they're just standing there. Like bloodthirsty predators, enjoying the fear of their prey before the mortal blow. The first Universal crumples to the ground, without a single Colonial having moved a finger. Everybody looks around. No one seems to understand what's happening. The second Universal drops. Like a felled tree. Then, the third, the fourth, the fifth. Our people start to panic and begin to aimlessly run here and there without having any idea where they're going. One after the other slumps. No blood, no screams, just a flock of sheep, penned in and waiting for the end. Without hope or fighting spirit. Rubio pulls at my jacket. "Quick. I know an escape tunnel."

I nod. From the corner of my eye I see someone taking aim at us. A woman is hiding behind a pillar. She raises an object to her face. It's a blowpipe. I step between Rubio and the woman. A searing pain shoots through my body. I pull the arrow from my neck. My vision clouds. A second later I'm on the ground. "Brick!" Rubio is calling my name. He seems to be very far away. I'm looking up to the dome of the U-Atrium and ask myself if this is the end. A woman leans over me. It's Zoe. Is she real or am I hallucinating?

25

Four Days Later
Colonial Territory, U-Atrium Checkpoint Charlie, Sub-Level 1

The day has 28 hours, that much is sure. The rest is hidden behind a wall of fire. This expression has become a popular catchphrase in New Berlin. The human race is flexible, that's what everyone claims. I found myself a place to sleep in a café. My mattress is right behind the bar. Here, nobody bothers me. There are no surveillance cameras either. We are allowed to move around U-Atrium Checkpoint Charlie freely. Why did the Colonials drug us and bring us here? I have no idea what to make of it. But I have the strange feeling that the worst is yet to come.

The Colonials are not like I expected them to be. The difference in looks is the first thing that catches the eye. Hardly anyone here wears the military-type buzz cut, common among us. Unlike us they sport a variety of hairstyles, the women often braiding their tresses. Colonials also try to express their personality by dressing in different styles and by wearing jewelry. Uniforms seem to be reserved for combat only. They're obviously not worried about a prisoner revolt, because if they were our guards would be armed. If I'm wrong, they must be good at hiding their sickle-blades from us. Maybe it's only a test to see how far we'll go. They still might crack down on us in case of disobedience.

Felicitas came to see me last night. She claimed she also was abducted during the raid, but somehow I don't believe her. I've never seen her at RAW before. Why did she pick the day of the raid to hang there? I suspect that Felicitas is a Colonial spy. Since we've had sex I know that she is twenty-five at the most. At Café Spreeblick she wore makeup that made her look older. What normal woman would paint dark shadows under her eyes and highlight her wrinkles? We're a society of forty-year-olds with Supervisors in their sixties. Nobody is in their twenties. Nobody but Felicitas. And Zoe.

U-Atrium Checkpoint Charlie has been cut off the subway system a long time ago. The tracks of the magnetic rail haven't been used in years, it seems. When Universal prisoners are led into the camp, they arrive on foot just like we did. According to my estimate there must be a little over two hundred of us by now. Rubio is not among them. I hope he was able to get away. We were the first prisoners to arrive here. Maybe Checkpoint Charlie is just a minor Colonial outpost. It might also be a camp for prisoners who don't pose too much of a security risk. There have to be more camps than this. Looking at the battles that took place during the last years, there must have been thousands of war prisoners. I'm sure they keep them somewhere else.

I'm surprised that they didn't transport us any deeper into the hinterland. To West City or even further than that. Away from the inner city ring. So close to the front we could turn out to be a threat to them. Acts of sabotage are one way to weaken the enemy. I, for my part, won't just sit here and twiddle thumbs, resigning myself to fate. I need to gather as much information as possible. Because I now understand, how little we know about the Colonials. I'll just let them think that they're dealing with a band of Outsiders and junkies here. Maybe I'll be able to lull them in a false sense of security.

"Stop complaining about the food, dumb bastard!" Cassio barks at a fellow-prisoner. Cassio already has made his peace with the new situation and is now reigning supreme over the food counter. He even has adapted his tattoo, turning the "U" into an inverted "C" with a patterned background. I wonder what he'll do, should the Universals take back the U-Atrium. "Only one ration each. And everyone will be nice and wait his turn." When Cassio recognizes me, he comes up to me, handing me a red ration. Blue, red, yellow, green, orange, there're all types of jellies to be had. No rules dictate what color has to be served on each particular day. How does Cassio know that red jelly is my least favorite one? The contempt in his eyes doesn't escape me. He seems to enjoy his new power. However, cozying up to the Colonials means that he's playing with fire. In case of a revolt, Cassio will be the first one to be lynched. But I guess he knows that. "You're a nobody here. Keep that in mind, Brick," Cassio hisses into my ear. "If you're not a nice boy, I'll tell them that you're one of them fucking headhunters." The human race is flexible. There's a grain of truth in that, I guess.

26
U-Atrium Checkpoint Charlie, Sub-Level 1

Remember. The inscription with our slogan on the wall has faded. It's been a little over three years now that the Colonials have taken U-Atrium Checkpoint Charlie. Since then no one has freshened up the larger-than-life letters. But at least they haven't been painted over. The Colonials show as little interest in us as they do in our slogans. Is it out of ignorance? No idea. At least they take care of our physical needs. Food is sufficient and the water supply works. But as much as I'd love to go outside, the Colonials won't allow it. We're not to leave the domed hall, that's the only rule they impose. The entire day we spend locked up inside the U-Atrium. We're not forced to work. There isn't any conditioning therapy either. We have nothing to do. Absolutely nothing. The days blend into each other in a dulling routine. Hell, I almost wish, they'd interrogate me. Is it their idea to break us with mind-numbing idleness? Until we succumb to lethargy? But never in my life will I collaborate with the Colonials. I took a solemn oath to myself never to surrender.

I've only spoken to three Colonials so far. I did so even though I was under the distinct impression that the men didn't want to speak to me. As soon as I opened my mouth, their eyes started to glaze over. They weren't downright rude, but definitely absent-minded. A little aloof, too. While my harpoon gun was taken from me, I was allowed to keep my dictating machine. This helps me to organize my thoughts. Not knowing whether the Colonial offensive has been warded off, bothers me. Was the enemy able to progress to U-Atrium Frankfurter Tor? I hope the northern front didn't get under pressure, too. Everything is in a flow, but I'm stuck here and at a standstill.

And I also noticed something else. The Colonials seem to have an aversion to physical touch, preferring to keep their distance not only to us, but also to each other. The guards at the camps are replaced every day. I use each changing of shift for my scouting expeditions, systematically exploring the tunnels that lead off U-Atrium Checkpoint Charlie. While the risk is high, the results so far have been more than sobering. The northern tunnel that would get me to U-Atrium Unter den Linden has collapsed, debris blocking my way. Like the domed hall at Alexanderplatz, the U-Atrium must have been destroyed during the explosion on Museumsinsel. Escaping to the west is impossible as well, as the Colonials have set up a checkpoint before U-Atrium Potsdamer Platz. A formation of marines decked out in tactical gear is a barrier even I can't get around. I'm unarmed and don't stand a chance against them. When we came here, we crossed U-Atrium Moritzplatz in the east. Therefore, I know that a number of Colonial companies are stationed there. This means I have to try my luck in the south. It's the only option open to me. However, I don't hold much hope.

Remember. Don't you ever forget. My comrades are too busy worrying about themselves. They can't be bothered to deal with the question how to best weaken the enemy. Life goes on, I hear them say. Every man for himself, they say. They all seem to have adjusted to the new situation. *Remember.* If I tried to share what I remember, nobody would care.

27

The Next Morning
U-Atrium Hallesches Tor, Kreuzberg, Sub-Level 1

The domed hall is deserted. Fungus lichens have devoured the walls, covering tables and benches like a second skin. I've problems breathing. Maybe the Colonials have set me up, and I have just walked into their trap. I can't return to U-Atrium Checkpoint Charlie, as by leaving the domed hall I've violated the only rule my captors established. I'm sure the Colonials punish this transgression severely.

When I cough I bring up black mucus. I need a short rest, before I continue. Just a minute or two to relax and gather strength. Yes, two minutes at the most. I cough. Again and again. The black mucus is now streaked with read. I need to lie down for a moment. Just to stretch my limbs. Nobody can blame me, right? I'll be fine again in a moment.

"I made it just in time."
Someone's talking to me. A woman. I'm on the ground. No idea how long I've been out.
"You're a strong-willed guy."
The woman continues talking at me, even though I don't answer. I don't know how long this has been going on. When I open my eyes, I see a blonde woman with a scar on her chin. C21 was right. Zoe has found me.
"You're different from the others." Zoe runs her hand through her hair.

I'm trying to get my head around what has happened. "Have you injected me with something?"
"If not, your body would have discontinued to exist."
The coughing has stopped and I wonder why. "What did you give me?"
"You would call it an antitoxin. It will make you immune to the fungus toxin for a while."
I sit up. "Thank you."
The corners of Zoe's mouth turn up. It looks as if she were attempting a smile without knowing how smiling really worked. She runs her fingertips across the fungus growing on the back of a chair. "A strange feeling. Even though I feel the fungus on my skin, I still remain myself."
I frown. "Are you sure you're all right?"
"Why?"
"Don't get me wrong, but you sound like you've taken Illusion."
Zoe rolls up the sleeve of her sweater, exposing a wound on her upper arm. The crust is still fresh. "Why did you hurt me?"
I realize that this is the wound I gave her at Schlesisches Tor. "It's my job."
"It is your job to hurt people?"
"I'm a headhunter. Sometimes I hunt killers. But mostly it's spies and traitors."
"I have never done anything to you."
When I want to touch Zoe with my hand to show her how sorry I feel, she shrinks back. "I really didn't want to hurt you. I just wanted to stop you from getting away."
"Is this supposed to be an apology?"

"Yeah."

"First, you do something bad, and then you say you are sorry?"

"I didn't want to hurt you."

"What other reason was there for you to do something evil like this?"

"I thought that you were Bull's killer."

Zoe runs her hand over the crust. Her eyes are shiny.

"My body heals."

"Why are you so young, Zoe?"

"I am not young."

"You're a very old soul, right?" I compress my lips. I'm rambling. Normally I'm not into this spiritual mumbo-jumbo. Not at all. This damn fungus is fogging my brain.

"I have spared you twice and saved your life once. Will you still continue to hunt me?"

"I don't know."

"There is so much violence in the hearts of your people."

I raise my brows. "Are you joking? You're the ones forcing this brutal war on us. You've been tormenting us for twenty years. And still you're accusing *us* of violence?"

"We are just attempting to restore an age-old balance. Something that has been missing for millions of years."

"Wow, it hasn't occurred to me that Colonials could have such noble motives. You might almost forget, while counting the bodies."

Zoe leans in. And then the woman who can barely manage a smile declares in proud tones: "We are not Colonials, we are rebels."

28

U-Atrium Hallesches Tor, Sub-Level 1

Zoe is the strangest woman I've ever met. Even by Colonial standards she's anything but normal. Maybe she's an outsider among her own people.

"Your name is Brick?" Zoe studies me.

"Yeah." I nod.

"Why are names so important to your people."

"The questions you ask. Maybe you'd better ask the computer. Do you have one here?"

"I have read the files. Now, I want you to tell me in your own words."

"Well, I'm not as smart as our central computer. But I'd say that names are part of our identities. They're quite practical, too. Just imagine that there are ten of us sitting at a table and you'd like me to pass you the soup. How would you do it without knowing my name?"

"I would point my finger at you."

"Well, that's a possible solution, I guess, but it's also rude somehow."

"Did your parents call you Brick?"

"No, Brick's my nickname. Something hit me on the head. My memory has been kind of shot since then."

"You have been hit on the head by a brick?"

"No, it was something else. I don't know what exactly."

"What makes you so sure it wasn't a brick, if you don't know what hit you?"

"Because we don't have any bricks in New Berlin."

"You are confusing me, Brick." A few seconds later Zoe's still shaking her head, as if searching for a gesture that goes with her words.

"It's a nickname I was given by others," I try to explain. "Nicknames don't have to make sense."

"And why did you keep it?"

"Because it fits me like a glove."

"Your name fits you like a glove, because it doesn't make sense?"

"Exactly."

"That is a paradox."

"You're pretty knowledgeable."

"I have access to the rhetoric module."

I frown. That means I'm literally creasing my forehead until it has more folds than the universe has stars. "And what about you? Why are you called Zoe?"

"That was the name on my coveralls."

"Wait a moment, you're losing me here. You call yourself Zoe, because that's what it said on your coveralls? Not because it's the name your parents gave you?"

"I don't have parents."

"You're an orphan?"

"No."

"What's this supposed to mean?"

"It means exactly what I have said."

"Okay, okay, I got it. We all have our secrets, haven't we? If you don't want to talk about it, fine. I'm just relieved that your coveralls didn't say 'Joe's Garage'."

Zoe ponders for a while. "Was this a joke?"

"I'm not very funny, I know."

"Am I expected to laugh now?"

"If you want to be polite, you can laugh, I guess. At least a smile would be appreciated."

"I want to be polite." Zoe turns up the corners of her mouth.

"Yes, pretty good. But your eyes need to be included, too. Not just the mouth. Your entire face. Like this."

Zoe studies my face expression and tries to mimic it. The result is a mixture of a smile and a concentrated frown. But I'm probably not a very good role model, as far as face expressions go.

"You mustn't interact with him." A voice booms through the domed hall. Zoe and I turn around. When Zoe sees the person approaching us, her smile disappears at once. It's a grey-haired man, who's wearing a toga-like garment. It looks like it's made from fungus lichen. In this hall the toga has the effect of a camouflage suit. "This man cannot stay here. He has to return to the others."

Zoe lowers her eyes to the ground. "You don't need to watch over me."

"You must not trust this Universal. He will just take advantage of your gullibility."

The man seems to be in his sixties. The same age as our Supervisors. This must mean that there are hierarchal structures among the Colonials, after all. If I just had my harpoon gun now. It could turn the tables of war to our advantage, if I managed to kidnap one of their leaders.

The old Colonial is glaring at me. "This man is thinking about ways to trick us."

Zoe shakes her head. "He is not like the others."

"Nonsense. He is infested with the same flaws. The same aggression."

"If it weren't for them we wouldn't stand a chance to restore the ancient equilibrium."

"How can we show weakness and still win the war?"

"Maybe this man is the key, Primus."

"I told you not to call me Primus."

"It is better to give you a name than to point my finger at you." Zoe smiles. Then she casts me a challenging look. I don't have a mirror to check my expression. But I think it's a smile Zoe has just conjured on my face.

29

On Colonial Territory, U-Atrium Kottbusser Tor, Kreuzberg, Sub-Level 1

I simply don't understand why we couldn't defeat the Colonials in all those years. They are so disorganized. They neither adhere to a daily routine, nor do they know sickle tournaments or boxing fights. What do they do to stabilize their sense of community? The Colonials must be hiding their true strength from me. Or is this really all they have to offer? Zoe openly answers my questions. Security clearance seems to be a foreign principle to her. But she also might be trying to fool me. It might be her job to present the Colonials as peaceful folk.

Train service between the U-Atriums has been discontinued. Therefore, we have no choice but to walk to U-Atrium Kottbusser Tor. There's fungus growing everywhere. The storefronts in the shopping mall are covered with lichen. Only the central fountain and the radial water ducts branching out from there have been kept clear. The closer we get to the front line, the fewer Colonials we meet. Besides some marines patrolling the U-Atrium, there is nobody around. It seems that the Colonials summon their troops from the hinterland shortly before each attack. Colonial life is probably very different when you get further away from the front. I can only speculate on this. As forthcoming as Zoe might be, she clams up when conversation turns to the hinterland. It's remarkable how the Colonials use the fungus as a natural obstacle. As we need the subways to move our troops, every foray would come to a quick halt. The information I gather here will be unbelievably useful for our military strategists and help them to plan the annihilation of our enemy.

I have to admit that deceiving Zoe makes me feel uncomfortable. Maybe I can convince her to change sides. Even though I know she's the enemy, I'm happy when I'm with her. Zoe is smart and unpretentious and has a disarmingly naïve approach to things.

"Why do you have so many shopping malls?" Zoe sits on a bench in front of the central fountain, dips her hand into the water, and watches the droplets bead on the skin.

"We like to consume."

"Consume?"

"Yeah, to browse in the stores and to shop. That's what makes us happy. However, this was long before the war. I honestly can't remember the last time the stores in the malls were open. Even though this doesn't necessarily mean much. My memory is like an Emmental cheese."

"Emmental cheese?"

"That's a cheese with holes like a sieve. Not that you could get this cheese in New Berlin. Or any cheese at all. Your blockade lines stop deliveries from getting through. What can I tell you? We make the best of it and use the stores as meeting places."

"But in the old days you used to go there to shop?"

"Yes. We earn Credits and spend them on nice things. That's the deal. One hand washes the other." I hold out my hand. Zoe doesn't understand that I want to shake.

"One hand washes the other?"

"Yes, that's what they say. It's called a...?"

"Metaphor?"

I snap my fingers. "Exactly, right. Blessed be the rhetoric module."

Zoe's face is stony. "You are laughing about me."

"No, I'm not. I want to laugh *with* you, not about you. That's a big difference. It wasn't a joke on your expense."

"Expense..." Zoe takes a deep breath. "This is all so complicated. I don't know if I will ever learn."

I want to put my hand on Zoe's shoulder, but draw back at the last moment. I know that Zoe doesn't like to be touched. "Just try to look at it this way. All of us are children of the evolution. Our basic needs want to be met. There are still the hunters and gatherers of yore in all of us."

"Evolution," Zoe thoughtfully repeats. "You are saying that you behave like this, because it ensured your survival in the old days?"

"What do you mean by *you*? All human beings are the same in this respect. Some are hunters, some are gatherers."

"Why do you gather?"

"You of all people ought to know the answer to this one, as you are the great gatherer here."

"What are you talking about?"

"You stole the artifact from Bull's antique shop."

"What artifact?"

"The artifact that was in the trunk. The trunk that was marked 'Icarus'. You stunned me and ran away with the artifact. Did you really think I didn't know?"

"It is not an artifact."

I frown. "What is it, then?"

Zoe clamps her hand over her mouth. "I am not supposed to tell," she mumbles almost unintelligibly.

"What aren't you supposed to tell?"

"It is a secret."

"Has Primus told you not to talk to me about it?"

Zoe nods. "No."

I smile. At least I think I do. "You have to work on your body language, you know? When your gestures and words are out of synch, it might make people wonder."

"That is what Primus said, too."

"Okay, so you can't tell me what the artifact really is. Can you maybe explain why you stole it?"

"I did not steal it."

I wave her off. "Please spare me. The lesson 'Lying 101' will follow tomorrow."

"A lesson is a unit of learning."

"Who else could have stolen the artifact?"

Zoe stares at me with widened eyes. She seems to be afraid. "The killer."

"You saw who killed Bull?"

"Yes."

I'm having trouble with the sequence of events inside the antique shop. "This means the killer came back after you stunned me?"

"You led him to the trunk."

I massage my neck. "Me?"

Zoe nods, yes.

"Who is the killer?"

"A human being."

"Could you be a bit more precise?"

"What are you talking about?"

"What does the killer look like? What's his name?"

Zoe takes her time. She seems to carefully choose her words. "I want to make a deal with you."

"Whoa, you're learning fast."

"I need your eyes, Brick. If you lend me *your* eyes, I'll tell you what *my* eyes have seen."

30
Deep Down Below New Berlin

The fungus worries me. How long will the effect of the antitoxin last Zoe has injected me with? Zoe doesn't seem to have a first-aid-kit on her. She carries neither bag nor backpack. I wonder where she got the hypos with the antitoxin from. I feel the need to cough again. The effect of the antidote seems to wear off. Zoe doesn't display any symptoms. She must be congenitally immune to the fungal toxin.

By now we've arrived below sub-level 5. According to Zoe we have to go down even deeper. The only ones who ever come down so far are the Diggers. There are neither walls nor tiles and I also don't see any metal or plastic. Just the fungus. My flashlight illuminates a tunnel system. The ceilings are so low that I can barely stand up straight. Our path meanders back and forth and continues to lead us further down on a slight gradient. There are so many turnoffs that I'm getting confused. At least we don't need oxygen tanks. The Colonials must have found a way to pump oxygen into the tunnels. An impressive feat of engineering.

Zoe knows these tunnels like the back of her hand. Again and again, I need to remind myself that she's the enemy. I hope she'll stick to her part of the deal. I'd never find my way back on my own.

"I feel like I'm in a labyrinth," I tell her. "What's the name of this mythical creature again, who lived in a labyrinth? Half human, half steer?"

Zoe thinks for a moment. "Minotaur, you mean?"

"Yeah, right." I nod in respect. "You're really well educated."

"I have studied your history."

"You know much more than I do."

Zoe puts her hand on my flashlight. "You can switch off the light now."

"Why? It'll be pitch-dark."

"Trust me, Brick."

I comply even though I've no idea what Zoe has in mind.

"Can your eyes see in the dark, Brick?"

"No, not a thing. Which was to be expected. Where would any light be coming from down here? A kingdom for a night visor! Then I'd maybe... maybe..." I stop. The walls begin to glow, alternating from red, to green, to purple. The pulsating light moves back and forth between the tunnel walls in perfect harmony like a school of fish. I've never seen anything like it. The lights remind me of Morse code. The pattern is definitely not random. If I didn't know better, I'd say we're dealing with an intelligence, which is trying to communicate with us. Zoe's face is bathed in a sea of colors. "There's an ancient prophecy among our people. Times of bloom will be followed by times of doom. Dark clouds will bank up in the sky and misery will rain down upon us. Beware of the advent of the monsters from space, who will sound the death knell of our civilization."

"Who are you, Zoe?"

Meanwhile, we've reached the end of a tunnel. Zoe is pointing at something. It's an eye scanner, almost overgrown by a mass of fungus lichen, the first sign of civilization I've seen for hours. "Can your eyes open this door, Brick?"

31

Back on Universal Territory, U-Hall Volksbühne, Mitte, Sub-Level 1

"Haven't I promised you?" Supervisor Stegner raises his arms. "Haven't I promised you that no distinctions will be made? We're all equals! We're all united! And nobody will escape their due punishment! Did you hear me? Nobody!"

The audience inside Volksbühne cheers. The man sentenced to death is standing on a stool. He wears a wire noose around his neck, his hands are tied to his back. He's a Supervisor like Stegner, who now turns his head to the VIP stand and bows. "We honor our fallen heroes."

"We praise and honor them," the crowd replies as one. Eva's company is among the guests of honor. The survivors that is, as the unit has suffered high losses. Eighty of the originally hundred marines have been killed, wounded, or taken prisoner. Eva is unharmed, thank God. I didn't have a chance to talk to her yet, because the guards don't allow anyone access. I'm standing on the balcony with Charlotte and Tom. The execution seems to bore Tom, while Charlotte is fidgety, adjusting her corset again and again. "It's this bastard's fault that we've lost three U-Atriums."

A nasty smile from Tom. "I don't mind RAW being gone. This way we got rid of this Outsider scum, at least."

"We've too many traitors among us. Universals who don't know where they belong." Even though

Charlotte avoids looking at me, I know that her barb is aimed at me.

Tom nods, yes. "Just give me the order, Charlotte. I can't wait to have a go at it."

Charlotte lifts her hand to stop him. "I still need corroboration."

"You know that our informer's reliable."

It's a strange feeling to listen in, while your own execution is the subject of negotiations. Does Charlotte know about my little outing to the Forbidden Zone? I can only hope that the Observators at U-Atrium Weinmeisterstrasse haven't been busted. Who else could have shopped me? I haven't heard from Rubio since we've been separated. Does Charlotte believe me to be a double agent, working for the Colonials? I'd better not tell her that I've been kidnapped by the enemy.

Applause surges up, when Stegner put his foot on the edge of the stool to carry out the sentence. The prisoner closes his eyes.

"Unity!" the crowd roars. Some voices can be heard above the others: "Burn in hell, dirty traitor!"

Stegner's taking his time, looking first at the sentenced man, then at the audience. He lifts his foot off the stool and walks a few steps toward the VIP stand. The prisoner seems to relax. Suddenly, Stegner whirls around, returns to the prisoner, and kicks away the stool from under him. The Supervisor is dangling on the noose. His name is Jens Baumann. He was one of the heroes, who brought the Colonial spring offensive to a halt by coordinating the resistance. But who cares about past glory? With Baumann dead, Stegner is now the head of all Supervisors.

"Unity!" the crowd cheers. Baumann twitches two times, then his body goes limp. The audience falls silent. For a moment the hall is deathly quiet. People are disappointed, because the execution was over much too fast.

"Don't worry!" Stegner reassures them. "Don't worry, there's more to come. The space cannon is standing ready. I'm sure our friends across River Spree are already waiting impatiently for our daily salute."

Laughter and hooting from the audience. Stegner points his finger at the banner behind the stage, lowers his head, and closes his eyes. "Never... do you hear me? Never must we forget who we are."

"Remember," the crowd answers as one, hatred turning into devotion as if someone had thrown a switch.

"Never must we forget what we are fighting for."

"Remember."

"Never must we forget who our enemy is."

"Remember!" People rise from their seats. Applause echoes around the hall. Charlotte reaches for Tom's hand, still avoiding my eyes. This time she doesn't ask Tom to take my hand, too. I watch the Supervisor swinging on the noose, thinking about another noose slowly tightening around my own neck.

32

Residential Tower "Semper Fidelis", Nordbahnhof, Mitte, Top-Level 4

I've never been to Toaster's place before. The ceiling of his penthouse is made of glass. Swathes of smoke like dark clouds glide across the sky above the residential tower. Even at an altitude of more than 260 feet you don't get to see a clear sky. Toaster has an indoor swimming pool, flanked by leather sofas. Water is a valuable commodity, its waste being strictly forbidden. Here, however, this rule doesn't seem to apply. To me it's obvious that Toaster's on the take. No doubt about it. There also is a round Jacuzzi, hidden behind plastic palms. It's been a long time since I've seen so much luxury. Toaster clearly belongs to the kind of people, Stegner routinely berates in his speeches.

I'd have never thought that I'd get to see Toaster in his home. Alas, I have no choice. I have to hand-deliver the Supervisor's killer to Charlotte as a proof of my loyalty. It's my last chance to save my neck. I have a deal with Zoe. I need to find a way to open this door in the sub-level, somewhere in the underbelly of New Berlin. In return Zoe will tell me what she saw inside the antique shop. The task is anything but easy. The eye scanner didn't accept my B1 access clearance. A2 or higher are required. I only know two Universals who have this clearance level. And asking Charlotte is out of the question.

Someone's sneaking up to me from behind. I don't move, keeping my eyes on the pool. I can't show fear now. No matter what Toaster has in store for me, I have to take it. I hear the sound of a toaster popping slices. Next, the phantom smell of roasted bread fills my nostrils. Toaster grabs me from behind. He's stronger than I expected. I don't even try to shake him off. Toaster presses the barrel of his gun into the side of my body. "First, you take out the Speedy's left kidney. Then the other." Toaster lets go of me. I turn to look him into the eyes. After adjusting his facial prosthesis, he points his gun at my chest. It's a CT305. I feel a shiver running down my spine. "And in the end," Toaster continues. "In the end you finish the Speedy off with a shot into his heart. Are you listening? Three rounds are enough to liquidate one of those bastards. You've seen with your own eyes what remains of them."

Thousands of thoughts are competing for attention in my head. But I have to stay calm. "This is a CT305, isn't it?"

"Not my favorite gun by far. At least you can still get ammo for it." Toaster deposits the gun on a coffee table. "If you miss the heart and the kidneys, these damned scumbags continue to live. Don't trust anyone, the enemy has infiltrated us. Even the P.I.D. is contaminated."

Toaster could easily have killed me if he had wanted to. I'm playing a dangerous game, but I need to make sure that I'm not barking up the wrong tree. Because suddenly everything starts to make sense. "*Monkey*

Killer. Weren't you the one who came up with this nickname for the serial killer of Charlottenburg?"

"Sounds good, doesn't it?" Toaster smiles. His asymmetric face never ceases to confuse me. "This guy offed his victims with his bare hands."

"Yeah, he was strong as a bear..." I hesitate and swallow. "Like you were... before... before you were seriously wounded during the spring offensive."

Toaster's eye darts over to where his gun is. "The Monkey Killer was a man to my liking."

"An incapacitated killer would never rely on his physical superiority alone. He would use a weapon instead."

Toaster nods. "We're all getting lazy with time. With the years you gain experience and status. The access to resources. Waning strength, but more power."

"This means that it would have become easier for the Monkey Killer to get hold of a weapon."

"There are plenty of weapons in the P.I.D. storage vault."

"And what about firearms? A CT305, for example?" I make a step in the direction of the coffee table. Where the gun is.

"A person like this would be able to get hold of such a gun, too." Toaster presses his hand against his prosthesis, even though it's firmly in place. For a while we stare each other down, both of us waiting for the other one to speak up first. To tell the truth about the serial killer who didn't only shoot Supervisor Neumann and Colonial C21, but has been murdering people around New Berlin for years. Who knows how many victims there are? We're eyeing each other, it seems to be forever, the gun on the table and within reach.

When Toaster realizes that I won't make the first move, he casts me a look filled with contempt. The untouchable one remains untouched once more. "I hate your guts, Brick, but you're not my enemy."

"You'll stay our hero, no matter what."

"Do you really think I still care?" Toaster brushes a strand of his wig off his face. "It's nothing to me!" he roars. "I don't give a shit about those fucking Universals!"

"Oh, keep your hair on."

"I've fought for my comrades. For nobody else! Do you really think I'd continue letting myself being hitched in front of the Supervisors' cart? Are you really stupid enough to believe the propaganda people like Stegner try to fool us with? Because if you do, the brick must have destroyed more than everybody thinks."

"But... what will remain, if we don't stand shoulder to shoulder?"

"Get out, Brick! Now!" Toaster walks over to the pool and starts to undress. It's not only half of his skull that has be replaced with a prosthesis. His right shoulder, his hip, and his left leg down to the knee consist of metal, too. I hadn't realized that his injuries were that severe. Toaster's skin is covered with scars. He also wears inked crosses all over his back. It must be hundreds of them. I don't even want to think about what they stand for. Toaster takes a dive into the pool, leaving his gun on the table.

33

Volkspark Hospital, Friedrichshain, Defunct Tract at Sub-Level 3

I'm getting sloppy. That's usually the beginning of the end. A headhunter's resolve must never falter. Now, I've broken this rule. For the first time ever.

"Drexler?" My voice echoes through the defunct tract of the hospital. Drexler must be hiding somewhere. It would have been my duty to give up Toaster to Charlotte. Then, everything would be fine. It would have bought me a lot of brownie points to bring her the man who is the Monkey Killer aka the Crazy Killer aka the murderer of the Speedies. What masterstroke it would have been to put the man on stage at Volksbühne. The success, Charlotte so desperately needs after the loss of the U-Atriums. But something stopped me from handing Toaster over. My instincts told me that the pieces of the puzzle didn't quite fit yet. Toaster could have easily killed me. Why did he first point a gun at me and then just put it on the table? I need to find out whether Toaster's CT305 is the same weapon that killed C21. Once I know the answer, I'll decide how to proceed.

"Drexler?" No answer. There's an x-ray image displayed in the light box on the wall. You don't need to be a doctor to see the tumors surrounding heart and kidneys. What was it that Toaster's said about Speedies? Three shots. Two to the kidneys, one to the heart.

"Drexler?" The trinocular is in place. I notice the shell case I found in C21's cell sitting in a dish. Where on earth is Drexler? I'm desperate to compare the two slugs. I point Toaster's CT305 at a locker and pull the trigger.

The shot rings out, but still no response. "Drexler? Are you here?" I study the shell case from Toaster's gun under the trinocular. The firing pin hasn't hit the percussion cap square in the middle, but left an imprint that resembles the letter C. There's no doubt about it: Toaster's gun is the weapon used to murder C21. When someone touches my shoulder, I jump.

"What are you doing?" Drexler's looking at me, suspicion in his eyes.

"Hell, must you sneak up to me like that? That's not your usual style."

"Why are you here?"

"I just wanted to check if the imprints on the shell cases are identical."

"Was it you who just fired a gun in here?"

I smile. "I banged up your locker a bit, sorry about that."

"As you seem to have finished your business, you might as well leave now." Drexler ignores my joke. I don't understand why, because normally he enjoys a banter.

"Are you okay?" I look at Drexler, who is as pale as usual. Drexler raises his eyes to the ceiling. "It's lonely down here."

"Lonely? And this from the most obstinate hermit under the sun? You seemed to be so happy, when they finally left you alone."

"I miss the bustle in the wards and my colleagues. And my job."

"How much longer will the suspension last?"

"I've made mistakes."

"Nonsense. You're an excellent pathologist."

"If I want to be admitted back into the Community, I need to repent."

"I must be hearing things. Are you really Drexler, the spirit that denies?"

"That's all past now."

"Are you sure you're okay?"

"The tumor in my lung is gone." Drexler doesn't sound happy.

"The x-ray in the light box? Is it yours?"

"Yes."

"Aren't these new tumors? In your heart and in your kidneys?"

"They're not tumors but the sites where the fungus germinated."

"Germinated?"

Drexler pulls up his pants. The wound on his leg has healed. "The fungus has formed three fruiting bodies inside me, encapsulating heart and kidneys."

"Shit! Does it hurt?"

"No, I don't feel a thing."

"Have you been to see a surgeon?"

"I've everything I need down here."

"Can't you have these fruiting bodies removed?"

"Removed?" Drexler looks at me incredulously. "Why should I?"

"You're asking me why? Are you serious?"

"If I did, the cancer would return."

"But you can't just leave it like this. How do you know what these fruiting bodies will do to your health?"

Drexler casts a nervous glance around the room. "Who else is with you?"

"Nobody. We're alone."

"You've brought someone along, didn't you?"

"No, I swear I did not."

"But these voices..."

"What voices?"

Drexler's expression darkens. "Have you reported to Charlotte Fleming already, Herr Hofstetter?"

"*Herr Hofstetter*? What's this bullshit? Since when...? What the hell is wrong with you?"

Drexler's eyes beseech me. "These voices… something… there's something happening inside my head."

"What can I do to help you?"

"I don't know."

"Maybe you'd better take your meds again. What was the name of these antibiotics again?"

Drexler's eyes widen. "What are you saying? Antibiotics?"

He pushes me away. "No!"

"Please let me help you!"

"No! No antibiotics!" Drexler's voice has turned shrill, he's starting to sound like a stranger. He glares at me. Only now I notice the scalpel in his hand.

34

Later that Evening
U-Hall Max Schmeling, Prenzlauer Berg, Sub-Level 1

I'm in possession of the murder weapon and I know the identity of the killer. Which means that I don't need Zoe's help anymore. I'm sure that Toaster was the man Zoe saw inside the antique shop. Toaster has murdered Bull and stolen the artifact. Toaster also is the killer of the Supervisor and of C21. He's been committing murders under my eyes all around West City. I just don't understand his motives. He's not the kind of serial killer who's driven by some perversion or the other. To him, killing rather seems to be an act of duty.

Drexler worries me. The fungus is growing inside his body, and that's not good at all. I've no idea how to help him. I also don't like the way he seems to be falling apart in front of my very eyes. Even though Drexler didn't downright threaten me with his scalpel, I found his hostile behavior highly disconcerting. I've never seen him lose control like this.

"Come on! Come on!" The people at the tables are egging on a couple to climb into the ring. Felicitas smiles. "Look, how the woman encourages the man to play along. Isn't it cute?" Felicitas is my escort for tonight. She also managed to escape from the Colonials. That's a reason to celebrate, isn't it? Felicitas has contacted me via the intercom and invited me to come along to U-Hall Max Schmeling. It suits me just fine. I want to have fun. Tomorrow, there will be hard decisions to be made.

The people at the tables applaud. The usual boxing fights have been suspended for a month; the hall will be used for a game show called "L-Gladiators" during that time. Couples sit at tables for two, which have been arranged around the ring. The plates in front of them are still empty, the waiting staff has yet to make its rounds. I hope we're not having red week. I so hate red jelly.

People cheer, when the chosen couple climbs into the ring. They're both very attractive, category-A material, that much is clear. The metal blades of the sickle spears that are placed into their hands now are covered in foam rubber. Four pedestals have been erected inside the ring. It's up to the woman to choose the couple she and her partner will be fighting against. A spotlight follows her index finger around the hall. The audience likes it that she takes her time. When she starts making eyes at the male members of the audience, her partner doesn't look very happy. Finally, she selects a couple sitting close to the ring. They're physically inferior to her, that's quite obvious. Category C, I guess. The man's prosthetic arm is limp. There must be something wrong with the stimulus transmission between his nerves and the prosthetic's hydraulic system. The A-man seems to come to the same conclusion I did, because his smile is triumphant. Armed with their sickle spears, the four of them take position on the pedestals. The bell for the first round is sounded.

"The Colonials don't have something like this, right?" Felicitas smiles at me. Again, she wears this terrible makeup that makes her look much older than in her mid-twenties. She seems to be nervous.

I nod. "The Colonials aren't really into having fun. I wonder how they keep up their morale?"

"That's an interesting question."

"How did you manage to flee?"

"I've got my ways." Felicitas thrusts out her breasts. "Whatever we might say about the Colonials, men are men. Everywhere."

I don't believe a word, Felicitas is saying. However, she seems to be able to shuttle back and forth between the cauldron and the occupied territories at will. There's only one possible explanation. But I won't deal with it tonight. Tonight I want to have fun.

The audience starts clapping. Both couples are grimly determined to win the fight. The C man is doing amazingly well. Even though he's hampered by his prosthetic arm, he's light on his feet, dealing his opponent blow after blow. The two women, too, are relentless fighters. When the A woman takes a swing at her opponent, the other one begins to reel, falling off the pedestal. The fight is over for her. People hoot and clap even harder. The A woman leaps over to her partner's pedestal, which means that the C man now has to fight both of them on his own. That's the rules.

If he manages to push the A man off the pedestal, he gets to spend the night with the woman.

When I try to catch Felicitas' eyes, she avoids my look. "Why do you think we can't win against the Colonials?" I ask.

"What are you talking about?" Felicitas blinks a few times. I notice that her breath frequency is going up. And that's not because of the fight.

"The Colonials don't have any troops standing at the front."

"Everyone knows this. Their army is deployed in the hinterland."

"Have you ever been there?"

"Been where?"

"The hinterland?"

"No."

"What makes you so sure then, that their troops are there?"

"That's what our leaders say."

"And if our Supervisors are wrong?"

"You're doubting our leaders?"

"If I were the one in charge, I'd launch a major offensive against the Colonials right now. Send everyone there, who's able to walk, to finally break the encirclement."

A wave of laughter surges up. The audience snickers. Soon, I see the reason why. The C man managed to shove the A man off the pedestal. Felicitas reaches for my hand. She still avoids my eyes. Her palm is damp from sweat. "Don't open this door, Brick," she says with a trembling voice.

35

The Next Morning
Residential Tower "Semper Fidelis" at Nordbahnhof,
Top-Level 4

Felicitas wanted me to take her home last night. But I gave her a rain check. I spent the night in the subway system instead, traveling from one U-Atrium to the other, randomly switching lines. Thinking. There's only one explanation why Felicitas knows about the door in the sub-level: Charlotte must have told her. But how? Has Charlotte gotten wind of my attempt to access the central computer? No matter how I look at it, there's just one person who can answer my questions.

The door to Toaster's penthouse is ajar. "Hello?" No response. I push the door open. Silence. I draw Toaster's gun. There are still eight rounds in the CT305's magazine. I tiptoe through the penthouse apartment. Water's softly lapping inside the pool. I notice someone in the Jacuzzi. But I can't see who it is, because the plastic palms block my way. "Jeremiah? Is it you? I came to return your gun. No idea what's gotten into me..." I get closer—and recoil. The water inside the Jacuzzi is red. Toaster's chest has been slit open. Blood is seeping from a deep gash. He's beyond help. The killer was skilled with his sickle blade, driving it into Toaster's body with enormous strength.

The door to the dressing room is open. "Show your face, bastard!" My request goes unheard. When I risk a peek into the room, I freeze. Toaster's little collection doesn't consist of clothes at all. Instead, I see rows of so called Consertainers, receptacles popular among storm troopers because they keep severed limbs fresh until the injured person can be transported to a hospital. Fingers and toes, eyes and noses, Toaster's stock leaves no wish unfulfilled. The Consertainers bear inscriptions in a neat, yes, almost pedantic hand: "Speedy Colonial 56", Speedy Colonial Hackesche Höfe 134" or "Speedy Colonial Rosenthaler Platz 162" the labels say. However, it looks as if Toaster hasn't only collected the body parts of Colonials. When I read "Speedy LN 213" and "Speedy PB 212", two Universals come to mind: Ludger Neuman and Paul Bull.

Toaster knew that he was playing a dangerous game. I wasn't his enemy, he said. Was the blood test the reason why Toaster spared me? I stare at the severed body parts in the Consertainers. How did Toaster manage to fool me and everyone else for such a long time? For twenty years he's trying to eradicate a phenomenon that was unnatural to him. Toaster was obsessed with Speedies. And it almost looks as if he wanted to pass his knowledge on to me.

I study Toaster's corpse: the prostheses, the tattoos, the scars. A tormented mind in a tortured body. Toaster's left eye is the real thing, the right one has been replaced with a glass orb. Felicitas has warned me not to open this door. There has to be a reason for it. Felicitas was nervous when she gave me Charlotte's message. Is it possible that Charlotte put her on me from the very start? She's stopped trusting me a long time ago. Maybe she just didn't fire me, because it would have jeopardized her standing with the P.I.D. I need to know what's behind this door. Whatever it costs me. I've heard that dead eyes can be used to trick the eye scanners. There's no such thing as a foolproof security system. This much is sure. Some of the Consertainers in the dressing room are empty. Toaster has to do me one last favor.

36
Forbidden Zone, Alexanderplatz

I take Rubio's route via U-Atrium Weinmeisterstrasse. The wail of sirens follows me all the way into the Forbidden Zone. General mobilization has begun, which means that I need to report to my commanding officer. If I don't do so within the next two hours, I'll be considered AWOL. I run a high risk, but I won't give up now. I want to find out the truth first. Zoe has been waiting for me below the TV tower. She leads the way, I follow.

The extent of devastation at Alexanderplatz also affects the lower levels. Even at sub-level 3 we come across bent struts and molten metal. The fungus is everywhere. The deeper we get, the denser the layer becomes. But I don't need to worry about the fungal toxin. Not as long as Zoe is with me. Some elevators still work, but most of the time we have to use the ladders inside the shafts. I do so with shaky knees. Before I start climbing, I try to calm myself by whistling a tune. I've confessed to Zoe that I'm afraid of heights. She doesn't seem to be bothered by the ladders, which she scales light-footed and without giving it a thought. What can I tell you? While Zoe needs to practice her smile, I have to work on my fears.

We make our way below sub-level 5. I don't need my flashlight any longer, because the glow of the fungus illuminates our path. When we reach the door at the end of the tunnel, Zoe gives me a challenging look. I remove the lid of the Consertainer and take out Toaster's eye. Zoe stares at me, aghast.

"I'm sorry, but I can't spare you this," I say.

"This eye belongs to the evil man."

"Evil man? What are you talking about?"

"The evil man is hunting us. He also did..." Zoe clamps her hand over her mouth. "I'm not allowed to say," she mumbles.

I smile. "I know this scary man. He's wearing a facial prosthesis and a wig. He killed Bull and then stole the artifact. His name's Jeremiah Glass, but everyone calls him Toaster."

"The evil man..."

"Well, maybe Toaster was crazy, but he wasn't evil. He also had his good sides."

"Our deal is finished. You know the truth."

"I don't give a damn about the deal. Why, do you think, did we come here?"

"Do you also want to open the door?" Zoe's face lights up. "Why?"

"For the same reason that made me come to a place that's called the *Forbidden Zone.*"

"I don't understand."

"Charlotte doesn't want me to open the door. There has to be a reason behind it. And I want to find out, what it is." I hold Toaster's eye to the scanner. "Charlotte will wonder how Toaster managed to come back from the dead." The laser scans the iris of Toaster's eye. A shrill signal resounds "Please try again," the female computerized voice says. I comply. "Second verification attempt failed," the computerized voice comes from the speaker. "You have one more try left, after which the emergency locking mechanism will be activated for eight hours."

"Damn, I had hoped the Consertainer would help." I look at Zoe pleadingly.

Zoe holds out her empty hand. "Let me give it a try."

"We only have one more stab. If it fails, we'll have to hang here for ages."

"Trust me." Zoe smiles at me. At least she's trying to smile. But even though her smile isn't a smile, I believe her. Carefully, Zoe takes Toaster's eye from my hand, studying it from all sides. Then, she starts to massage it with her fingers. I don't understand what she's doing. "You have ten seconds left to confirm your identity," the computerized voice intones. Zoe holds Toaster's eye in front of my face. "Can you see for me one more time, evil man?" The eye's pupil contracts, as if Toaster had come back from the dead.

37

Forbidden Zone, a Sub-Level Deep Down Below Alexanderplatz

Toaster's eye has opened the door to an unknown world. We step into a sleeping cubicle that hasn't been entered for ages. Everything is conserved like in a time capsule. A fine layer of dust has settled on the furniture. And somehow the fungus, which rules supreme in the sub-levels below Alexanderplatz hasn't been able to take hold here. The cubicle's interior design is very different from everything I've seen in New Berlin: cold colors and plain forms dominate the space. The impression is functional, stripped down to the bare necessities. The closet contains a uniform. The epaulets tell me that it belongs to an officer. The cufflinks bear an inscription: "Icarus".

Zoe walks over to the desk. I watch her opening one drawer after the other. "What are you looking for?"
Zoe takes a box from one of the bottom drawers, placing it on the desk. "Patience." Zoe opens the box. I see a cylindrical object, about the size of a ball pen. The object looks like Bull's artifact, the only difference being that there are three golden rings worked into the base instead of four.
"What's so interesting about these artifacts?" I ask.
"These aren't artifacts."
"What else could they be?"
"Keys."
"They don't look like keys to me."

"Do you see the lines engraved into the metal?"

"Yes, of course."

"It's not a random pattern."

"I figured that much. What is it, then?"

"A verification code."

"A code? What for?"

"It's the code that starts the machine."

"Machine? What machine?"

"The machine that has dropped on our planet."

"A spaceship, you mean?"

"I mean Icarus."

"You say, Icarus is a spaceship?"

"Icarus came from space."

"Wait a minute. Are you actually saying that... that this cubicle here... that we're aboard the Icarus?"

"The Icarus split up, before it collided with our planet. We're aboard a daughter ship of Icarus."

"We are... Icarus split up... what are you talking about?"

"I tell the truth."

"When is this supposed to have happened? Just look at the metal. Absolutely no rust. This means the cubicle can't be all that old. While the space ship must have crashed a long time ago. That means long before New Berlin was established."

"It wasn't a crash but part of a plan to conquer a new world."

"Bull never mentioned a space ship. And Bull knew what he was talking about. We discussed his artifact a lot."

"But Bull had no idea that it was a key. When I heard that Bull had one of these keys, I wanted to talk to him."

"But Toaster beat you to it."

Zoe nods, yes. "The evil man killed Bull. And you led him to the key."

"I didn't do it on purpose. I thought Toaster had already left."

"I need to restart the machine, Brick."

"Maybe you're telling the truth. Honestly, I've no idea what this weird place is. But you also have to understand why I'm a bit skeptical. There are so many urban myths around. In the sub-levels people talk all day long. About dead bodies putrefying within a few hours. About people, who take a bullet in the heart and don't die. And don't forget the rumors about a mythical underbelly of New Berlin. About people vanishing without a trace. And now you're telling me about a spaceship that crashed a long, long time ago." I look at the ceiling, trying to calculate how deep down underground we might be. "And New Berlin was built on top of the crash site?"

"You will believe me when you see the truth with your own eyes."

"It just doesn't make sense. The eye scanner opening this cubicle is definitely one of ours. How else could we have unlocked this door?"

"You just do not understand the entire picture, Brick."

"Even if this cubicle really is part of a spaceship... looking at the Spartan furnishing, I guess it's a battleship, right? But if it is, how could it still be possible to start the engine after all this time?"

"The machine has been activated once already after the landing. However, there was a functional error. If I succeed in restarting the machine and repair the problem, the program will be completed."

"But that's... how... how do you know all this?"

"The files say so."

"Of course, what else could it be? The *files*..." I stare at Zoe. Has she completely lost her mind, or have I underestimated her all this time? Was I wrong to mistake her lack of social graces for simple-mindedness?

"Okay," I say. "Let's assume that it is a key. How many keys do you need?"

"Four."

"And let's also assume that this machine really can be started, as you claim it can be. What for?"

"I want to create a new world."

"Well..." I take a deep breath. "You're never at a loss for words, I have to give you that. But if you..."

Zoe raises her hand. Suddenly, she is absolutely focused. She looks over to the door; she must have heard something. "We are not alone," she whispers. I draw my CT305 and point it at the door. Eight rounds. That should be enough for a welcome party.

38
Flak Tower at Humboldthain, Top-Level 1

Visibility is lousy due to the smoke. But still I've everything in my sights from atop my perch. Only one shift at the flak tower, then I'll be excused. I made it back from the Forbidden Zone just in time. Zoe will wait for my return at the TV Tower.

The wreckage of the last battle is scattered along the bulwarks that guard our northwestern border. I'm sure the Colonials aren't quite as strong as our leaders want to make us believe. To defend your borders, you need to keep watch over the entire front, while the attacker has a free pick where to launch the next battle. The Colonials make good use of that advantage by concentrating their forces in a few places. In my eyes they're more like a band of guerrilla warriors than a regular army. It's high time for us to force their hand.

"Saved by the bell, Brick." Eva comes up to me. She's wearing her dress uniform. "Your commanding officer was just about to report you AWOL."

"Well, what do they say? We all need a little luck sometime." I hug Eva. We keep silent for a long time, our thoughts being everywhere but in the here and now. "Have you been moved here?" I ask Eva eventually.

She nods, yes. "We need to regroup. We had too many losses."

"Damn."

"They have lumped three companies together now and send us to this place to regain our bearings." Eva's eye starts to twitch. "It's quiet here, right?"

"The Colonials need a break. Just like we do."

Eva peers through the bulletproof pane of our crow's nest. "Remember, Brick, the Colonials control the hinterland, while we only hold the cauldron."

"The Colonials are worn out like we are, believe me. I have myself..." I compress my lips.

"What did you do?"

Eva's not supposed to know that I've been kidnapped by the Colonials. "I've heard rumors," I answer instead, "that the Colonials, too, are desperate. Losses are much too high on both sides."

"The older generation is slowly stepping down, Brick. It'll be our turn to replace them soon."

"The time hasn't come yet."

"I hope you're right, Brick. Toaster's dead, did you know?"

I keep a straight face. "Impossible. The man has seven lives."

"No, no, it's true. Toaster's finished. I've heard it from different sources. People say he had his throat slit in his penthouse. By a headhunter."

"Who does?"

"You know how rumors circulate in the sub-level. You just repeat it often enough until it sticks." Eva studies me, a question in her eyes. "You don't happen to have anything to do with it, right?"

"Me? Whatever gave you this idea?"

"I heard that someone..."

"What exactly have you heard?"

"Well, some people say... it's just gossip, mind you, but there's talk that you... well, that you weren't 100% loyal."

I cross my arms in front of my chest. "They doubt my loyalty, I see. After all I've done for the cause?"

"It's only a few who think like this."

"How comforting. And what do *you* think?"

Eva averts her face. "I think that you're one of our best men, but..."

"But what?"

"Brick, you just aren't... what's the best way to put it? You've changed."

"I'm still the same person."

"Neuman's murderer's still at large. Things like that never happened to you before."

As much as it rankles me to have her take me for loser, I can't tell Eva that Toaster is Neuman's killer. I need to assemble the parts of the puzzle first. "Who, do you think, has spread these rumors?"

"Take a guess."

"Charlotte?"

"Fleming is getting a lot of flak. Stegner wants to do some restructuring in the management level of P.I.D."

"You want me to tell you what loyalty is? What it feels like to put loyalty above everything else? Do you know who my haul No. 96 was?"

"You've captured so many."

"It was Jack Schneider."

"The Supervisor, we've just..."

"Yeah, him. I attended his execution by space cannon on Charlotte's orders. This was her way of telling me that I'll be next, if I don't toe the line. It's bad enough that she doesn't trust me. And now you..." I notice Eva staring into space, a dazed expression in her eyes. "I'm sorry." When I take her in my arms, I feel that her entire body is trembling. Even though she tries to put on a brave face, the last battle has taken its toll. War sooner or later even catches up with the best of us. What did Zoe mean when she said she wanted to save the world? Could this possibly apply to both parties, Colonials and Universals?

39

Forbidden Zone, TV Tower at Alexanderplatz, Ground-Level

I sit on a picnic blanket, a glass of wine in my hand. River Spree slowly flows by in its bed. "We'll give up everything we have," someone says. The voice is that of a woman.
"A new beginning," I agree, turning my head. But it's not a woman who raises her glass to me. Next to me on the blanket, there's an alien creature. It has the shape of a human being, however, with all parts being out of place. As if someone had turned everything inside out. Its skin is just a finely woven net of blood vessels and neural strands. "We'll populate this new world," the creature with the voice of a woman says. Next, someone touches my shoulder. "Wake up, Brick, we need to go."

I need some time to come to. Zoe's sitting next to me, legs crossed. "Your eyes were moving, even though your eyelids were closed."
"Yes. I had a dream." I sit up. We've met in a maintenance room in the base of the TV tower. The room is dirty and reeks from oil.
"What was your dream about?"
"Oh, just crazy stuff."
"Why do you people dream?"
I dust off my coat. "You people? You sound as if Colonials never had dreams."
"I'm not a Colonial."

"Yes, you've already told me. However, there are only two kinds of people, Universals and Colonials. And as you aren't a Universal, you must be a Colonial."

"Why do you have dreams, Brick?"

"Well, I'm not an expert, but I would think we do it to work things through. Things that occupy our minds."

Zoe considers this. "There are things that occupy my mind, too, and still I don't dream."

I yawn. "Lucky you. This means you don't have nightmares either."

"But I'm curious what it's like to dream."

"Maybe you actually do dream and just can't remember it."

"Is this possible?"

"Yes, it happens more often than you'd think."

"It's a weird system to first work things through and then to forget right away that you did."

"Well, it wasn't my idea."

Zoe stands. "The time has come, Brick. I will now let you in on my secret."

"Does this mean you finally trust me?"

"I know now that we're on the same side."

I rub my neck, feeling guilty. "I want to be completely honest with you, Zoe. Don't even try to pull me over to your side, because it won't work. I'm a Universal. To the core."

Zoe smiles at me. Even though her smile isn't a smile, I know that she doesn't take me seriously. "If you're a Universal, how come you're here?" she asks.

"What are you talking about?"

"Are you allowed to enter the Forbidden Zone?"

"No, of course not."

"In this case you've violated the rules of your community."

"Well, more or less... technically speaking... but I'm doing it for the common good."

"You've informed your people of your plans, you mean?"

"I... yes... well... no, not yet."

"Why not?"

"What do you think? Because I first had to find out what's going on here."

"See, that's one thing we have in common. I also didn't tell anyone else what I'm doing here."

"You're looking for these keys on your own?"

"The others wouldn't understand."

"And you trust me because I haven't told my people?"

"We're rebels, both of us."

"Bullshit, I stick to the rules."

"But not a hundred percent."

"I'm not perfect."

"I like you not being perfect." Zoe walks over to the door of the maintenance room. "And now come."

"Where are you going?"

"Up."

I scratch my chin. "Up?" I repeat, not liking the idea. "Up into the tower, you mean?"

"Yes."

"Is this really necessary?"

"What's wrong?"

"I assume that the elevators aren't working. Which means we'll have to use the ladders."

"There's a stairwell going up."

"An open stairwell?"
"Yes, for emergency evacuations."
"Oh, great."
"I like the tune you're always whistling..."
"... whenever I'm scared of heights?"
"Yes."
"Now you're putting me on."
"I want to laugh with you, not about you. That's an important difference."
"Well, well..." I fail to suppress my grin. "You're a fast learner, Zoe. I have to give you that."

40

Forbidden Zone, TV Tower at Alexanderplatz, Top-Level 10

"Here we are." Zoe puts the key with the three golden rings into the lock.
"What? No eye scanner this time?"
Zoe shakes her head, no. "There's another security mechanism at work in this restricted access area." I hear a beep. The steel door opens.
"Since when is a viewing platform a restricted access area?"
"What do you mean by viewing platform?"
"Aren't we in the cupola of the TV tower?"
"We're on the bridge."
"Bridge? What bridge?" I look around. Control panels have been arranged in three concentric circles around a swivel chair. Daylight bathes the room in a warm reddish glow. In the sub-level we have to make do with the cold bluish light of luminescent diodes and neon tubes.

Top-level 10. The TV tower is the highest elevation in New Berlin. I can hardly believe that we have an unobstructed view up here. The black smoke that enfolds the city in a nebulous shroud is way below us. Above our heads, the sky is clear and blue.
"Come, I want to show you something," I hear Zoe calling in the back.
"Just give me one more moment. I haven't felt the sun on my skin for such a long time. Even if it's only through bulletproof glass." When I hear a beep from

behind, I turn around. Zoe is activating the control panels with her keys. I follow her to the swivel chair in the center of the room. "This is, where the fourth key goes," Zoe says, pointing at the aperture in the armrest.

"The key with the four golden rings?"

"It's the captain's key."

"And the other three keys belonged to his officers?"

"Yes. I need the captain's key to start the machine."

I shake my head in confusion. "Artifacts, which are actually keys. Machines that have to be started. The control room of a TV tower, which really is a bridge. I have to admit that you've lost me here. I've no idea what's going on."

"Maybe this will help you understand." Zoe points her finger at a brass plaque on the back of the chair. "Your people have built all of this, Brick. Don't you get it? It's your ship."

"Our ship? How can this..." The inscription on the plaque makes me stop.

"Remember. Remember where we came from. We came from aboard the Icarus. Remember what we are fighting for. We are fighting for a chance to populate this planet. Remember who we are. We are Colonials.

Captain and Officers of the Pioneer Ship New Berlin, Daughter Ship of the Colonist Cruiser Icarus."

41

Universal Territory, Residential Tower "Eberswalder Strasse" at Mauerpark, Prenzlauer Berg, Top-Level 1

"How much did they pay you?" I take a look around Felicitas' apartment: inviting and elegant, maybe a little too close to the front line. "It seems to have been worth the trouble."

When Felicitas tries to greet me with a kiss, I duck away.

"You were gone so fast last time," Felicitas says. "I almost believed you didn't like me anymore."

"Why, Felicitas? I need to understand."

"What are you talking about?" Felicitas sits on the couch, crossing her legs. She's wearing a robe and looks tired.

"How many Credits has Charlotte promised you?"

"Who's Charlotte?"

"I simply don't get it why you lied to me."

Felicitas twirls a strand of hair between her fingers. "I thought, we'd take up again where we stopped last time." She opens her robe. Her breasts are perfect.

"Why are you still so young?" I ask.

Felicitas yawns. "I just keep well."

"Bullshit. You're in your early twenties. How is this possible?"

"You wouldn't understand, Brick."

"Why not?"

"Will you excuse me for a moment?" Felicitas points toward the bedroom. "I need to put my makeup on."

"To look older than you really are?"

"You definitely have to work on your flattering skills, Brick." Felicitas laughs, but I feel how tense she is.
"Just go ahead," I say. "Go. You're not my hostage."
When Felicitas notices my eyes following her on her way to the bedroom, she sways her hips lasciviously. She locks the door from inside.

Universals and Colonials, pioneer ships and colonist cruisers. What's going on here? I massage my temples. The deeper I get involved in the secrets of New Berlin, the less I understand. I hear a voice coming from the bedroom. It's not the voice of Felicitas. After a few words, the voice becomes muffled as if someone had turned down the volume. I tiptoe over to the door to listen.

"I've already told you, he knows everything," Felicitas whispers. "You need to come here now. Brick's going to kill me... no, he's capable of anything... hurry up... please... you need to come here right now..."

I draw my CT305 and kick open the door. Felicitas is standing in front of the intercom. I point the gun at her head. "Tell me what's happening here!" I demand. "Why did you betray me?"

Felicitas theatrically drops to the ground. "Please don't shoot me!" she pleads, trying to protect her face with her hands.

"Speak up!"

"You have to understand. I had no choice. What was I supposed to do?"

"Has Charlotte put you on me?"

"Charlotte has been blackmailing me. She wanted... she has trained me."

"Trained for what? Spying?"

"I did it for my brother."

"Your brother? Who the hell is your brother?"

"He's still down there."

"Down? What are you talking about? Down in the sub-level?"

"Down in the hall."

"Don't try to bullshit me." My finger curls around the CT305's trigger.

"It's the truth, I swear."

"What did Charlotte offer you?"

"She'll wake my brother if I do what she wants."

"What the hell are you saying?"

"He's my brother. Charlotte wants to wake him like she woke me."

"Have you totally lost your mind now?"

"It's the truth. Charlotte has cleared the access to a remote dormitory two years ago. There are more than one thousand intact cryo-chambers there, she says. I was in one of them. You must understand. My little brother is still down there. In a cryo twilight sleep."

42

Hospital at Volkspark, Friedrichshain, Defunct Tract on Sub-Level 3

I press the CT305's barrel against my forehead. The cold metal cools me. Tom won't stop, until he's hunted me down. During the subway ride I have taken care to cover my face. I can only hope that the Observators haven't spotted me with their surveillance cameras.

"Is it time now?" Drexler comes up to me.
"Time for what?"
"Are you here to get me?" He points at the gun in my hand.
"Just a precaution." I pocket the gun. "I'm happy to see you joking again."
"Why are you surprised?" Drexler replies with a mischievous smile.
"The last time we met, you weren't in such a great shape, I must say. You were paranoid and aggressive. I feared for the worst."
"Which would be?"
"I don't know, but this fungus... I was worried this fungus might make you crazy."
"Well, you're not that far off the mark. It was, to sum it up, an incredibly astounding scientific experiment on myself."
"Are you serious?"
"You don't believe me?"
"Why did you get better?"
"I took antibiotics. More specifically, antifungals."

"So you took them after all. Last time you adamantly refused antibiotics because you were afraid that the cancer might return."

"Let's say I've settled on a compromise. I'm also still taking immunosuppressants to ensure that a bit of the fungus will always remain."

"Are you saying the fungus is still inside your body?"

"I need to play for time. As soon as I've found out how the fungus works against cancer, I can develop a cure."

"I'm happy to see that you're feeling better."

"I need to keep a balance between the growth of the fungus and the growth of the tumor."

"You're really a special person."

My compliment obviously embarrasses him. "Let's stop talking about me. What's new with you?"

"I went to the Forbidden Zone with Zoe."

"Who's Zoe?"

"The woman I was shadowing."

"I see."

"Did you know that all of us started out as Colonials?"

"So what?"

"You knew all along?"

"Universals, Colonials, the eternal struggle against evil. Do you believe this propaganda? Politics is politics, Max, you of all people should know."

"We were up in the TV tower. The motto on the captain's chair didn't mention any enemies."

"I had no idea you could still go up there."

"Is this all you've got to say?"

"Don't bite my head off. I'm a scientist, not a politician."

"Do you think that we can make a difference?"

"Depends on the intended result."

"Zoe has a plan. She wants to start this machine."

"What machine?"

"Honestly I've no idea. But Zoe is convinced that by starting the machine we will save the world."

Drexler laughs. "I definitely need to meet this woman, who has bewitched you into wanting to start a machine without knowing what it is good for."

"Her name's Zoe."

"Yes, you've already said so. It still doesn't explain why you want to save the world all of a sudden."

"There has to be a way out of this misery, Drexler. We've been fighting each other without mercy for twenty years now. What for, may I ask?"

Drexler studies me. "You have changed, Max. I just can't tell yet if it's for the better or the worse."

"We need four keys to start the machine. Three we found, one is still missing."

"And where is this fourth key?"

"Do you still have access to the autopsy suite?"

"Officially I don't. But there's a back door."

"Let's go. We don't have time to waste."

43

Hospital Volkspark, Friedrichshain, Autopsy Suite, Sub-Level 2

"Sooner or later they all end up on my table." Drexler gazes at the body on the autopsy table.

"Toaster was a killer," I say. "Neuman, C21, Bull, and dozens of others are dead because of him. Toaster had a collection of body parts in his penthouse. You'd be thrilled to see them. He used Consertainers to stop them from putrefying."

"These things are hard to come by. Even the storm troops have problems getting any."

"Is this all you have to say?"

"Do you expect me to be surprised because P.I.D.'s into committing murder?"

"I'm with P.I.D."

"That's why you know exactly what I'm talking about." Drexler studies Toaster's prostheses. "I have to admit that I've never seen anything like this before. And I'd assumed I'd seen it all. Half of his body is metal. The man must have been in a lot of pain."

"Toaster was obsessed with Speedies." I look at Drexler. "To him they weren't human beings but repulsive oddities."

Drexler takes his time answering. "I've experienced first-hand how the fungus can spread inside our bodies. And what it does to us. A couple of days ago I would have sworn that this Speedy thing was just a hoax."

"And now?"

"Now I'm not so sure anymore."

"Toaster's not a Speedy, that much is sure. His body still is in good shape."

Drexler nods. "Why did you want to see his body? To make sure he hasn't disintegrated into goo?"

"Toaster has collected body parts of all his victims. Maybe to study them, maybe as trophies." I lift the corpse to show Drexler the tattooed crosses on his back. "Toaster wanted to keep in touch with his victims. Look here, for each of them he had a cross inked."

"Wow, that's sick."

"Where would Toaster keep a key that's a souvenir of one of his victims?"

"Depends what the key looks like."

"It's a metal pin, not much longer than a finger, with fine engravings and four golden rings."

"Metal is best stored with metal where it won't stick out."

I stare at Toaster's prostheses. "Do you think...?"

"A metal pin won't attract attention if it's embedded in a metal prosthesis."

"I can't see any key."

"Let me have a closer look at his false leg. Maybe we'll find something that doesn't belong there." Drexler tests the stability of the prosthesis with a pair of forceps. "A metal pin could be hidden in the metal struts."

I look around. "Where's Dr. Todt, by the way?"

"Oh, he's just having a medal awarded to him at Volksbühne. Vanity, vanity."

"I can't stop wondering why someone with such a name can work as a pathologist."

"You're repeating yourself."

I scratch my neck. "Can I ask you something?"

"Shoot."

"What do you know about the netherworld?"

"The netherworld? Do you mean the sub-levels at the very bottom?"

"Do you think that there are halls down there, no one has ever set foot in?"

"Why do you want to know?"

"I'm wondering what you might find, if you just venture down deep enough?"

"Leave this work up to the Diggers."

"Aren't you curious what's down there?"

"There's nothing but the fungus."

"Maybe there's also the answer to the question where we come from."

"We live in the present, Max. Let's focus on that."

"Maybe the past holds the key to a better future."

"Might this be the key you're looking for?" Drexler pulls a metal pin from the prosthesis. Four golden rings, a fine engraving. It's the captain's key. Next, I hear a hiss that makes me recoil. The arrow from the harpoon hits Drexler square in the forehead, its line encircling my neck before I have a chance to react. Drexler drops to the ground, I land on top of him. The noose around my neck tightens. Someone jumps on me. "Two in one go," a man's voice murmurs close to my ear. I know whose voice it is. Tom's. The bastard must have followed me to the hospital. I manage to close my hand around the CT305 in my pocket and blindly fire behind me without taking it out. The pull on my noose slackens. Gasping for air, I push Tom off my body. Then, the world turns black.

44

Hospital at Volkspark, Friedrichshain, Autopsy Suite, Sub-Level 2

The arrow is embedded in Drexler's forehead. I feel for a pulse at his throat. Nothing. His body is cold. Rigor's setting in. How long have I been out? Drexler still holds out his hand as if to give me the key. The key, however, is gone. I close Drexler's eyes. Only now I realize that he was my friend. I need to avenge his death. Tom will pay dearly for this.

I notice traces of blood on the tiled floor. Half-dried droplets that have turned a deep shade of black. They form a trail, leading out of the autopsy suite. I must have hit Tom. Great. I survey the scene like a predator, sniffing out the scent of his bloodied prey. Focused and without mercy. I check the magazine of my CT305. Seven rounds left. Time to finish the job.

Where did I go wrong? How did Tom know that he'd find me at the hospital? I got away from Felicitas' apartment before the storm troopers arrived. Has Tom been lying in wait in the residential tower? When I see the pool of blood in the corridor, I'm yanked back into the here and now. The blood is smeared as if someone fell and picked himself up again. Tom. I recognize the imprints of his prosthetic legs. Those of his hands, too. Tom must be seriously wounded. The trail of blood ends at a locker nearby. I raise my gun and open the door.

Tom's skin is ashen, his eyes are closed. The bullet has entered the side of his body close to the left kidney, shattering the right one on its way out. A through-and-through wound. The CT305 has unleashed its destructive power to the maximum. Tom must have squeezed himself into the locker on his last ounce of strength to hide from me. It fills me with satisfaction that he spent his last moments in pain and fear.

When I search Tom's body, I don't find the key. Without the key I can't return to the Forbidden Zone, where Zoe awaits me. Staying in the cauldron isn't an option either. I can't trust anyone. I'm sure that Felicitas wasn't the only spy Charlotte has sicced on me. Where is this key? Tom's prosthetic legs are made from carbon fiber. Impossible to hide anything there. When I take another look at Tom's body, I make a startling observation. Within the last seconds something has changed. Tom's skin isn't pale anymore but has taken on a reddish sheen. I touch his forehead and find that he's burning. Can dead people come down with fever? Next, Tom himself answers my question. His eyes open and he shoves me away with so much momentum that I land on the floor. Tom leaps out of the locker and starts running down the corridor. Why isn't he dead? Nobody can survive a serious injury like that. The prostheses catapult Tom's body into the air. I shoot at him but miss. His movements are smooth and well coordinated. I take a second shot. Again, I miss my target. Tom reaches the door at the end of the corridor and is gone.

45
At Sub-Level 5

I follow the trail of Tom's blood deep down into the sub-levels. Fungus spores make it hard for me to breathe. I feel the effect of the antitoxin wearing off. How come Tom's still standing up straight? The bastard must have lost almost six pints of blood. He's probably drugged up with Illusion to the eyeballs not to feel the pain.

"U-Atrium Alexanderplatz" a sign next to a ladder says, an arrow pointing up. It's the first landmark I've seen in a long time that's not grown over with fungus. Why did Tom flee into the Forbidden Zone? Does he want to use the key himself? But he needs the other keys to start the machine. I start to cough. My phlegm is black as tar. My lungs are filled with fungus spores. I feel my throat starting to constrict. The antitoxin has stopped working. I need to get out of here. Now.

Slowly I clamber up rung after rung. The shaft looks familiar. I've been here before with Zoe. It's the central shaft under the TV tower. Sub-level 3. Zoe's waiting for me up in the maintenance room. I need to get there, no matter what it takes. Only three more levels. My knees are trembling. My strength is waning, as if my fear of heights weren't enough. I can't tumble down into the abyss. I leave the shaft at sub-level 2. The fungus growth here isn't as dense. Gasping for breath, I sit on the floor next to the door of the elevator. Panic starts to get hold of me. I lie down on my side and begin coughing again. Black phlegm lands on the floor. More coughing fits rack my body. I feel as if I'm about to bring up a lung. I cough and cough until I pass out.

"I'm happy I've found you," someone says. The voice is familiar. I open my eyes. Zoe's sitting next to me, legs crossed. "I've heard you cough all the way up." She smiles. It's the sweetest smile I've ever seen, even though no one else in the world smiles like Zoe.
"You've saved my life the second time," I say. I'm surprised that I've no problems speaking. "Do you always have antitoxin on you?"
"I haven't given you any drug."
"I don't understand."
Zoe leans in as close as she can without touching me. "I myself am the antitoxin," she whispers.
Even though I still don't get it, I know that she's saying the truth. "I'm so sorry. I almost had the fourth key."
"What happened?"
"Toaster... the evil man, I mean, he had it."
"And then he didn't have it anymore?"
"Tom has stolen it."
"Who is Tom?"
"Tom is a headhunter just like me. He has killed Toaster and Drexler. I shot the bastard, but somehow he's still alive, even though his kidneys are gone."
"I see." Zoe leans her head against the wall, squeezing her eyes shut. She seems to be thinking hard, trying to come up with a plan. "You should have also shot him in the heart."

"In the heart? What are you talking about? That's the way Toaster killed Speedies. Three shots, two to the kidneys, one to the heart."

"You destroyed two of his fungus bodies, which means that he has one more left. That's all he needs to regenerate."

"We have to get him. Now. Tom doesn't have much of a head start. He wants to gain access to the TV tower, I think."

Zoe shakes his head. "No, he needs to go back."

"Back? To the Colonials, you mean?"

"No, back to the origin, Brick. He'll try to make it to the Outer Ring."

"To the Colonial hinterland? Why?"

"There is no Colonial hinterland, Brick. The Outer Ring, this is where the realm of the mycelium begins."

46

Outer Ring of New Berlin, Grunewald, Ground-Level

We follow Tom's trail through a landscape strewn with debris. The imprints of his prosthetic legs can be easily made out in the dust. West City has been destroyed all the way to Grunewald. Ruins jut up from the rubble like stumps, the trees resemble skeletons. There is no Colonial hinterland, no land of unlimited resources the enemy can draw on. I also don't see any troops, not even patrols. In New Berlin's outer ring there is nothing but the fungus, dust, and black smoke that obscures the sky. We aren't kept under siege by a powerful enemy, after all. The truth is that we never were. The story was nothing but propaganda the regime used to keep us under its thumb.

"You need to dig a bit." Zoe sits and crosses her legs. "You'll hit water after a while." Zoe uses her hand to remove the layer of dust. The soil has been entirely replaced by fungus.

"Are you crazy? The water is polluted. The last time I had some of it I suffered from horrible hallucinations."

"Oh, dear. What did you do?"

"I took a crowbar and..."

"Violence is not the way it works." Zoe shakes her head. "Did the fungus bleed?"

"It oozed a white substance, if I remember right. I have to admit that I had a total blackout."

"You hurt the fungus, Brick. And the fungus retaliated." Zoe starts digging with her bare hands.

"You have to do it like this. Very gently." The shallow she digs fills with water. "The liquid is very nutritious."

"Well, I'm not sure about this. The stuff almost killed me. If it hadn't been for Rubio... Do you know Rubio?"

"No."

"Rubio is an Outsider. He told me that most people who ingested some of the fungus died."

"Where is Rubio now?"

"No idea. I lost sight of him, when you took over RAW."

"I hope you see him again."

"Me too."

"Do you trust me, Brick?"

"I think I do. You saved my life twice, after all."

Zoe takes up water with her hands and sips. "It tastes wonderful. A little sweetish maybe, but not too bad."

"What made you so sure that Tom would take exactly this route?" I look at the imprints Tom's prosthetic legs left in the dust. "He could have run north, I mean. Or to Tempelhof."

"This is the only possible way."

"To get to the mycelium?"

"Tom needs to go to the ocean."

"This is where the realm of the mycelium is?"

"Yes."

"And this ocean is supposed to be near here?"

"Yes. Northwest from here, just behind Grunewald."

This makes me smile. "I must have missed the deluge, then."

"What?"

"Since when is there an ocean behind Grunewald. Last time I looked, the Havel was just a river."

"You will understand when you see it with your own eyes."

Zoe blinks. Suddenly, her face is bathed in light. The layer of smoke breaks open and the sun appears. "The sunlight is wonderful."

I shade my face with my hand. "I haven't felt the sun on my skin for such a long time."

"Do you like it, Brick?"

47

Outer Ring of New Berlin, Beyond Grunewald, Ground Level

The ground reflects the sunlight, a glare that makes me squint. I can't see any fungus and also gone is the layer of dust that showed us the imprints of Tom's prosthetic legs. We've been walking on a shiny metal surface for a while now.

"We've lost Tom's trail."

"Don't worry. We'll get there in a moment." Zoe walks a few steps ahead of me. "Are you coming?"

I'm so utterly confused. We've crossed a field of debris, only to end up in a wood of dead trees. The cover of smoke has broken, the sun came out, and now the ground is made of metal slabs. "How much longer?" I ask.

"We're almost there."

"What's this realm of the mycelium supposed to be?"

"I've found the word in your files. The term mycelium is the closest approximation."

"Of course, the files. What else could it be?"

"You have to see it with your own eyes, Brick. You won't understand otherwise."

"Hey, I'm trying, right? But you know why they call me Brick."

"Something hit you on the head, but it wasn't a brick."

I smile. "You haven't forgotten."

"It wasn't me who was hit on the head, right?"

"Now you're making fun of me."

"No. I want to laugh with you, Brick. That's a big difference."

"Yes, of course."

Zoe looks me into the eyes. "When we find this headhunter, what are you going to do with him?"

"Tom has murdered Drexler. He's going to pay for this."

"Will you kill him?"

"We'll see."

"Have you killed someone before?"

"I've always delivered my customers to the P.I.D. alive."

"But the people were executed later, weren't they?"

"They all ended up in the space cannon eventually. It was decided by the Community. Traitors have to die."

"The world I come from is not like yours, Brick."

"Don't even try. I don't understand a word you're saying anyway."

"You need to accept that you are in a different place now, Brick. You still cling on to the place you left a long time ago."

"Don't try to confuse me."

"Have you never asked yourself, why trees don't have leaves in New Berlin and why the buildings are ruins?"

"What's there to ask? There's a war going on, and wars destroy things. And the plants wither away, because the smoke blocks out the sun."

"Have you never asked yourself, why your civilization only exists in the sub-levels?"

"We had to seek shelter down there because of the war. Besides, we don't only live in the sub-levels."

"There are no bricks in New Berlin, Brick. You said so yourself."

I have to think of the wall of the building near the Urania World Clock. I couldn't get through the layer of fungus, no matter how hard I tried. "The fungus has spread everywhere."

"There was nothing here before, Brick."

"Bullshit. We have buildings. We have residential towers and also flak towers to defend ourselves. There are the domes of the U-Atria. And don't forget the TV tower."

Zoe kicks the ground. "Your buildings in New Berlin are made of metal."

"The houses have been bombed to pieces, the landmarks are ruins."

"It wasn't you who built these houses, Brick."

I scratch my neck, feeling sheepish. "As I've already told you, I don't understand a word."

Zoe smiles. "In this case, I'll show you, Brick."

48
At the Edge of New Berlin

"Do you feel the energy?" Zoe gazes at the ocean, where a greenish and red aura is floating. "Can you see the flashes? These are bacteria. They supply the mycelium with energy."
"The color reminds me of the tunnel in the Sub-Level."
"The bacteria store up energy in the sunlight. Later they are transported down into the depths by the mycelium. To a place where the sun never shines."
"You've told me it was an ocean. Where's the water?"
"The mycelium has absorbed the water like a sponge."
Light flashes zing through the ocean like constant gunfire. I realize that the pattern isn't random.
"Is the mycelium intelligent?"
Zoe looks into my eyes. "There are cells that communicate with each other the same way your neural cells do."
"How big is the mycelium?"
"The mycelium rules over the entire planet, Brick. From the North Pole to the South Pole. There's no place without mycelium."
"And the fungus in the Sub-Level below New Berlin?"
"Is part of the mycelium."
"Is this mycelium a fungus?"
"That's the terrestrial life form it has the most in common with. But the mycelium exists on a much higher plane of development."
"And what's the part of humans in this game?"

Zoe smiles at me. With this very special smile of hers. "You need a little more time to understand."

"If the mycelium is the ocean, the edge of New Berlin is the shore."

"What do you mean?"

"The ocean, the beach, a man and a woman. Didn't your files say anything about it?"

"Do you want to...?" Zoe gives me a challenging look.

"Do we want to take a walk along the seashore?"

"Like two lovers?"

"I've read about romantic walks on the beach."

"Romantic... I haven't heard this word in a long time." I gaze at the ocean, the play of colors, the flashes of light. "Which way do we want to go?"

"What direction could the headhunter have taken?"

"North?"

"Okay."

"You think, Tom can swim?"

"He'll stay on the shore."

"What makes you so sure?"

"He'll try to save the body he lives in. That's what all of us want..." Zoe looks me into the eyes. She doesn't seem to be sure how to finish the sentence. "... all of us..."

I wave her off. "Save yourself the trouble. I won't understand anyway."

"You will when the time has come."

"Mold with a brain," I mumble.

"According to the files the mycelium rather resembles a slime fungus."

"Slime fungus? It just keeps getting better."

49

At the Edge of New Berlin

Tom is on the ground. He looks like a floater. His body is bloated, threads of fungus cover his skin. I'm surprised he even made it here in this state.

"Is he dead?" I ask.

"No." Zoe shakes her head. "The mycelium has established contact with him. He's regenerating."

"He'll be like he was before, then?"

"The human cells that have died will remain dead. The fungus will replace the damaged tissue as good as it can, taking over its functions."

"No matter what Tom is or what he's going to change into, for me he's still the killer of my friend." I draw my CT305, pointing it at his heart. "Two to the kidneys, one to the heart, just like Toaster said."

"Wait." Zoe blocks the muzzle with her hand. "If you destroy the last node, there will be nothing left of him. Then everything he was will be erased."

"Tom didn't need to kill Drexler. He did it out of sheer bloodlust."

"Killing him will change you, Brick." Zoe lowers her hand. "I have read in the files that you people have a conscience. Your deeds haunt you. People who kill are evil. I don't want you to become an evil person, Brick."

"I owe it to my friend." My shot hits Tom square in the heart. Or whatever has taken over its place in his body. Zoe lowers her eyes, but she doesn't say anything. When I want to touch her arm, she recoils.

"I had to do it," I try to explain.

Zoe still doesn't answer. Her eyes are red.

"Listen to me. I had to kill Tom. There was no other way." I remember the prophecy Zoe has mentioned before. "When you talked about people you didn't mean human beings, right?"

"I chose the term people, because you are familiar with it," Zoe says without looking at me.

"We human beings are the monsters your people are afraid of, aren't we?"

Zoe lifts her head. "Dark clouds will bank up in the sky and misery will rain down upon us. Beware of the advent of the monsters from space, who will sound the death knell of our civilization."

"And we human beings are these monsters?"

"From North Pole to South Pole there is no place without mycelium. Its network fills the entire planet, connecting everything with everything. Then, you humans came. And with you there was again a place without mycelium. To me, humans aren't monsters. Just the opposite. You have reestablished an age-old balance, reaching back into a past when the mycelium didn't rule our planet. You've brought us war, but also liberation. The harmony we've been living in all these millions of years, it doesn't create change. The mycelium knows one structure only. Its threads extend always in the same way. You human beings have inspired us. We have built houses in New Berlin, created buildings, reinvented ourselves."

"Whoa, wait a minute! You mean to say that the streets, the bridges, the grey facades, the landmarks, everything is your work? That's ludicrous." I sit on the edge of New Berlin, dangling my feet over an ocean made of fungus mass. What's this alien planet I've somehow ended up on?

"There's something new growing on the colonist platform New Berlin, Brick. Something that hasn't been here before. But the mycelium wants to stop it from happening. You need to understand, Brick. We are on the run from the mycelium. It's eating its way through New Berlin from below, pushing us more and more toward the center. We are rebels, looking for shelter in New Berlin. We're asking for asylum, as you humans call it."

50

At the Edge of the Colonist Platform New Berlin

"I'm sorry our romantic walk had to end like this." I'm staring at Tom's body. Putrefaction is happening in fast-forward mode.

Zoe turns away. "Why haven't you asked me yet if I'm like him, too? What do you call us, Speedies?"

Tom's features dissolve in front of my eyes. For a moment a human skull appears, disintegrating as quickly as it has come. I look at Zoe. "I don't care what you are."

"You won't kill me, then?"

"Kill you? What makes you think such a thing?"

"Because the evil man killed us. And you have his gun."

I look at my CT305. How many rounds left? I forgot counting. "It's not your problem that I've killed Tom, right? You're actually afraid I might turn into someone like Toaster."

"You have killed, Brick. And it will change you."

I stare at the mycelium ocean. "Do you know what you mean to me, Zoe?"

"You've never told me."

"I've never told you what you mean to me?" I raise my arm and hurl the CT305 far into the ocean. Lightning flashes, where it enters the mycelium.

Zoe smiles. In her very special way. "This is what I mean to you, Brick?"

"Didn't you know?"

Zoe averts her eyes, clearly embarrassed. That's something I've never seen her do. "I was hoping I did," Zoe says.

I feel my face redden. "Now back to work." I kneel in front of Tom's putrefied remains. "Tom has to have this last key on him. I'm sure he does. It's not in his pockets, I've already looked. But maybe..."

"Maybe what?"

"Maybe the key is... well... inside Tom."

"You think he swallowed it?"

"No, it's too large to swallow. I think, Tom has... ahem... he has put it in a place where things usually come out."

"Are you sure?" Zoe covers her mouth with her hand. "I still haven't quite gotten used to defecation. That's a really odd solution to the problem you humans have devised."

"Defecation? That's how you call it?" I smile at Zoe. "You'd better turn around. It's going to get pretty yucky now."

51
Rebel Territory, Inner Ring, Mitte, Brandenburger Tor

We've run into a rebel patrol at Tiergarten, but otherwise nobody showed any interest in us when we crossed the Outer Ring and West City.

"How does the fungus know what an antique pillar looks like?"

"The framework cells of the fungus grow the way we tell them to." Zoe looks at me from the corners of her eyes. When I look back, she turns away.

"And how do you communicate with them? You don't carry a remote control with you, right?"

"The air is filled with our proteins and peptides that maintain communications with the framework cells."

"And all these buildings in New Berlin? They're really made only from fungus?"

"You built the domes of the U-Atria, the residential towers and the defense towers, as well as the solar panels and the control tower. There was nothing else on the platform, when you arrived."

"I've always thought the buildings were buried under fungus, oil, and dirt."

"Why?"

"Don't take it personal, but the Brandenburger Tor and the facades of the buildings don't look all that realistic. They seem to be somehow melted and blurred around the edges. Have you seen in your files what the streets of old Berlin originally looked like? The colorful houses, the lights, the vitality?"

"Everything takes its time, Brick. Just wait a few centuries, and things will be perfect."

"A few centuries? How long do you usually live?"

"We don't define the individual like you do, Brick. Within the mycelium, our thoughts and memories will stand the test of eternity."

"And if you live in a human body?"

"You've seen what happened to the headhunter."

"There's nothing left of Tom."

"He's a thing of the past. And everything he was went with him."

"He left us the key, at least." My laugh is cynical. "His legacy, one could say."

"You were right."

"I hope we'll manage to start the machine now."

"We have all four keys."

"There is one thing I still don't understand. In New Berlin the fungus is growing like some kind of gigantic termite mound. But it isn't part of the mycelium?"

"No. The fungus on the colonist platform isn't controlled by the mycelium."

"Why hasn't the mycelium reached from the edge of the platform into the center yet. I mean, why does it take the detour via the sub-level? Why the complication?"

"In New Berlin the fungus can only survive thanks to the blanket of smoke. In the sun it'll die."

"Oh, that's why the edge is fungus-free?"

"Exactly. The sun makes the fungus wither."

"But the mycelium is exposed to the sun all the time. I've seen it with my own eyes."

"Don't forget that it's in the ocean. The water protects it from desiccation."

"Just one more question. What's the mycelium's problem with you rebels? Why are you on the run?"

"The mycelium resents separatism. It demands unity."

"Wait a minute. This more or less means that the mycelium thinks the same way we Universals do."

"Do you now understand what kind of war you're fighting?"

"A war of humans against non-humans?"

"No, that's not it. We also have humans among the rebels. The same as some Universals are hybrids, too."

"Hybrids!" I clap my hands. "Now, you finally told me who you are. I would have thought that you'd call yourself a fungus-person. But hybrid doesn't sound bad either."

Zoe raises her brows. "Are you making fun of me?"

"Yes, and it's about time I did. It's been my turn for a while now."

Zoe shakes her head. "You're acting like a child, not like a grown man."

"Small wonder, considering our difference in age. Remember, I'm in my early forties, while you must be thousands of years old."

"Are you... what do you people call it? Are you messing with me?"

"Don't be mad, okay?"

"I'm not mad." Zoe opens a hatch, leading down to the sub-level.

"What? Down again?"

"We need to, if we want to get past Museumsinsel."

"Give me a second." I look down the magnificent boulevard Unter den Linden. On Museumsinsel the eternal fire rages like a volcanic eruption. The sun is hidden behind a pitch-black layer of smoke. I can't help it, but this familiar inferno makes me feel at home somehow.

52

Forbidden Zone, Sub-Level 5, Below Museumsinsel

Pipes and support lines are covered in lichen. Zoe doesn't seem to need any clues to find her way around the sub-level.

"Why exactly do you want to start this machine?" I ask.

"Trust me, Brick."

"I do trust you. But what if it's a mistake to start the machine? What if it just makes everything worse? I'd love to hear more about your plan."

"Once we're on the bridge, I'll explain everything."

"Just a little hint."

"You need to be patient."

I start to cough. "Dammit, it's starting again."

"Come closer." Zoe looks me into the eyes. "Just stay calm. What you're feeling right now is the influence of the mycelium."

My breathing rate goes up. I try to stifle the rising panic. "I need the antitoxin. Now. Please."

Zoe comes very close, albeit without touching me. "I exhale the antitoxin from my lungs, Brick."

I gasp for breath. "Give it to me... please!"

Zoe blows air on my face. "As long as I'm with you the toxin can't harm you."

I feel like someone inhaling an asthma spray. "Is the fungal toxin the reason why so many Diggers just disappear?"

"Diggers?"

I take a deep breath. "You must have met them at RAW. People who go treasure hunting below ground."

"Human beings can't survive the toxin for very long."

"The Diggers have gas-masks with special filters."

"Do these people roam below sub-level 5?"

"That's what Rubio said."

"The tunnels below sub-level 5 weren't dug by human beings, Brick. The accesses and underpasses are constantly changing. There might be a dead end, where there was an open passage only a week ago."

"Meaning that a human would inevitably get lost?"

"Only hybrids can survive in these tunnels of light."

"So, Rubio's pals didn't stand a chance?"

"Why have these people exposed themselves to danger to begin with, Brick?"

"Us humans, we're pioneers. We're attracted by the unknown."

"That's what I like about you people, Brick. You just set out on your own, even if you don't know what's in store for you."

I smile at Zoe. "Sometimes we also form double-teams."

"Yes. That's what I like even more about you human beings."

"Why do you know your way around the sub-level below Museumsinsel so well?"

"Do you want me to show you a special place?"

"What place are you talking about?"

"The place I was born, Brick."

53

Forbidden Zone, Sub-Level 5, Below Museumsinsel

Row after row, block after block. It's impossible to tell how many cryo-chambers have been arranged side by side inside the hall. Zoe brushes the dust off one of the glass cylinders in which a person can be put into deep-sleep. "In this place I came to be aware of my body."

I notice the fungal threads, hanging like cobweb from the hall's ceiling. "Are the cryo-chambers controlled by the mycelium?"

"No, the fungus growing here is, like the one up on the surface, a renegade offshoot of the mycelium. But in the other halls the mycelium rules."

"How many of these halls are there?"

"More than one hundred. Plus, the five halls for the ship's crew."

"The chambers are empty."

"The people inside have been woken up."

"By the computer?"

"We are the ones who brought these people back to life, Brick."

"Have I, too...?" I wipe my hand over my face. "Have I, too, been contaminated?"

"Everybody carries the fungus inside them. But that doesn't necessarily mean that a fungal node has been formed."

"What are you talking about? What the hell does it depend on?"

"The fungal threads grow through your skin. What happens then, depends on the individual's health status. We can only take hold of ill people. People whose immune system has been weakened. Or people who are seriously injured."

"Injured?"

Zoe points at a cryo-chamber whose glass-cylinder is broken. "The landing was harder than planned. Not everybody survived the impact. Many people were injured. Seriously injured."

"That means there were problems?"

"According to the files it was a blind-date mission. The destination was supposed to be determined automatically during the voyage. But when Icarus approached our planet, the first irregularities arose. The central computer tried to wake up the crew, but failed. It couldn't establish contact to the crew-members inside the cryo-chambers. The multiple-redundancy emergency systems all malfunctioned."

"Must have been a hell of a security concept."

"Icarus had been in space for too long."

"What do you mean?"

"Icarus had been traveling for 900 years, when the probes finally located a planet that seemed to be fit for colonization."

"900 years?"

"Icarus split into several parts as planned. But the colonist platform called New Berlin collided with the planet surface with too much speed."

"What happened then?"

"The central computer autonomously started the pioneer program."

"Pioneer program?"

"The colonist platform was meant to serve as a base unit for the colonization of the new planet. It should provide provisions and infrastructure, ensuring the survival of the colonists during the first decades. Energy supply was secured with the help of solar panels and nuclear fusion reactors. Deep drills started an autonomous search for oil immediately after landing."

"And why was the whole thing stopped?"

"The search for oil was successful. However, a main pipe on Museumsinsel had been damaged by the hard impact. One spark was enough."

"And this one spark triggered the fire on Museumsinsel?"

"Yes."

"Why didn't the central computer just shut off the pipe?"

"The central computer tried to remedy the irregularity, but failed."

"And since that day the fire on Museumsinsel has been raging, fed by the underground oil well?"

"The central computer is waiting for human intervention."

"How did the fungus manage to enter the cryo-chambers? I'm not an engineer, but I'd think the chambers must be sealed."

The fungus was able to pass through the cryo-chambers' bacteria filters. We have developed an infiltration system. First, a protein spear penetrates the filter. These spears are only a few nanometers in width. Then, the diameter of the spear increases, and, one by one, fungus cells are sucked into the widening gap."

"And you reached the sleeping halls first?"

"We rebels are pioneers, just like you humans are. However, the mycelium made it to the first cryo-chambers shortly after we did."

"For twenty years, Zoe. For twenty years we've been fighting this war." I lower my eyes. "This war was never the war of the colonists. We've been fighting your war, Zoe. For twenty years we've been fighting your war."

"I'm sorry, Brick. I'm so sorry."

54
Forbidden Zone, Sub-Level 5, Below the TV Tower

"Do you know who the woman was, whose body you took over?"

"Zoe was a scientist. A botanist. Her body was severely injured during the landing. She wouldn't have survived."

"Is this your excuse for occupying the body of a stranger?"

"Other than you humans I don't know the concept of moral qualms."

"Lucky you."

Zoe looks down on herself. "I appreciate the gift this wonderful body is."

"You've just told me that everyone is contaminated, but not in all cases fungal nodes are formed. Is this infection the reason why there aren't any children being born?"

"Might be."

"How old are you? I mean, how old is your body? You look quite young."

"I was woken up two years ago."

"So you're in your early twenties?"

"All the colonists were around twenty when they set out on their journey. It is the perfect age for humans to discover new things."

"And the Supervisors?"

"They were the crew members of the colonist ship and in their forties when they started out. The perfect age to be a leader."

"Was Toaster a crew-member, too?"

"The evil man was the first officer of the New Berlin."

"The first officer. Is this a joke? I don't believe it! That's why the eye scanner recognized his eye?"

"It was a lucky coincidence that you came back with the eye of the evil man."

"Well, I wouldn't call it just a coincidence. I already knew that Toaster had the highest access clearance possible."

"I don't want to diminish your effort."

"I can't get my head around that Toaster was the same age as the Supervisors. His wig and prosthetics made it hard to guess how old he really was. I can't even remember what he looked like before he was wounded. Is your Primus also one of the crew-members?"

"Yes. Primus was the captain of the New Berlin."

"The captain? Wow! Toaster and Primus, what a team of princes."

"Primus was the first one woken by the fungus. This was thirty-five years ago."

"Was Primus alone at first?"

"Primus was the first and only one. Twenty years ago he launched the Great Awakening."

"What's the Great Awakening?"

"Primus woke up the people in seventy sleeping halls."

"Hybrids, you mean?"

"Humans and hybrids, Primus didn't make a difference."

"Stop finding excuses. You guys take over our bodies without asking first. That's not a nice thing to do."

"We have no choice, Brick. The same as you didn't have one when you killed the headhunter."

"The same as... I...?" I frown. "My reasoning was really pathetic. I only realize it now."

"We weigh our different options before we make a choice."

"The right choice, I assume."

"The only possible choice."

"Self-criticism seems to be a foreign concept to you. A bit of humility wouldn't hurt, I think. Don't take it personally, but the rebels I've met so far all came across as rather arrogant and aloof."

"We have these wonderful minds. And now we've also got these wonderful bodies. It went to some people's heads, Brick. But I'm not like this. I don't look down on you."

"Are there any halls that haven't been entered yet?"

"Yes, there are."

"Those people should be given the choice if they want to continue life as hybrids."

"Once the mycelium has had its way, there won't be any choices to be made." Zoe regards me. "The mycelium will annihilate all human beings. You, too."

"Why didn't Tom go down to the sub-level straight away to make contact with the mycelium? Why the detour to the edge of New Berlin?"

"The headhunter wanted so save his body. Only the ocean offers the necessary regenerative powers. Inside the light tunnels you run the risk that the process of regeneration might take too long. In this case the mycelium would absorb the fungal nodes."

"Do you mean to say that all hybrids, that is on both sides of the front lines, don't want to give up their human bodies anymore?"

"I can't speak for all hybrids, Brick. But as far as I'm concerned, I don't want to go back."

"Even if it means that you'll die like Tom did?"

"Let's talk later. We've lost enough time already."

"If you insist. But I'm still waiting for an answer." I peer up the elevator shafts. "Ladders seem to be my destiny."

Zoe looks at me expectantly.

I raise my brows. "What? Do you want me to whistle again?"

"That would be nice. I like this melody very much."

"If it makes you happy."

"Brick?"

"Yes?"

"Your face is all red."

"What?" I take a look at my arm. "A sunburn. Damn. This is really a sunburn."

"A sunburn?"

"I must have just caught it on the platform. How was I supposed to know that I needed to bring suntan lotion?"

55

Forbidden Zone, Inside the TV Tower, Ground-Level

"Do you hear this?" Zoe whispers.

"Yes." I recognize the black uniforms of the P.I.D. "We're not alone." At least ten police officers have taken position in front of the stairs to the tower. "It's useless," I say. "We'll never make it past them." We duck into the maintenance room we came to use as a meeting place. By now I regret that I've tossed the CT305 into the mycelium ocean. "And the elevators are really out of order?" My question sounds desperate.

"The shock wave after the explosion has warped the guide rails."

"Hell!"

"Someone must have gotten wind of our plans. What other explanation is there? I've come here hundreds of times without anybody waiting at the stairs."

I nod, yes. "I'm absolutely sure that Charlotte's behind it. Only the head of P.I.D. can authorize an expedition into the Forbidden Zone. Tom must have found a way to inform her. But how did he do it? He didn't have the time to use an intercom."

"The headhunter was in contact with the mycelium."

"So what?"

"The mycelium knew what the headhunter was thinking and therefore anticipated our actions."

"Does this mean that Charlotte Fleming is a spy?"

"You know what it means, Brick."

"I don't know anyone, with the exception of Toaster maybe, who's as absolutely committed to the

Universal cause as she is. She'd never... Charlotte could never... she has..." I start stammering. Suddenly, I understand what Zoe is talking about. It all makes sense. Charlotte wanted to neutralize the killer of the Speedies. At all costs. Not to help the Universal cause but for the one and only reason that she feared to be discovered and killed by the same criminal.

I'm yanked out of my thoughts by a deafening racket. Zoe and I tiptoe out of the maintenance room to find out what's happening out there. People scream, bark orders, and holler obscenities. Sickle-blades clang and a volley of shots rings out. The police officers are involved in a skirmish. I don't believe what I'm seeing. An assault squad of our marines is fighting the P.I.D. There must be a lot of open scores to be settled. I've rarely witnessed such hatred before. The marines obviously have not forgotten the many years they had to put up with being bullied by the internal police. When the police officers withdraw from the staircase, the marines follow in hot pursuit.

"This is our chance!" I look at Zoe. "It's now or never!" We leap across dead bodies, police officers and marines alike. The ground is strewn with severed hands, arms, legs, and heads. This wasn't the choreographed hate routine, cultivated between Colonials and Universals. It was purposeful annihilation. When we rush up the stairs, our feet clatter on the metal steps.

"Brick!" The scream is shrill and filled with hatred. Like a curse, the sound of my name follows us and catches up with us on Top-Level 1. "Brick!" It's a voice I really hoped I'd never hear again. Zoe turns to look at me. For the first time ever I notice something akin to fear in her eyes.

56

Forbidden Zone, Inside the TV Tower, Top-Level 5

"Brick!" Charlotte doesn't give up. She's tenacious. One of her most prominent traits. I'm out of breath. Zoe runs ahead, light on her feet. Where does she take this strength from? I can't keep up with her. "You've got the key," I gasp. "I stay here and delay Charlotte."

Zoe stops. Now, it's only one person's steps echoing on the metal steps. Charlotte will catch up with us any minute.

I take a deep breath. "I'll delay Charlotte... stop her..."

Zoe looks me into the eyes for a moment. Then, she turns and starts running. I sit on the stairs. About five seconds later Charlotte arrives and stops in front of me. Her first reaction is to flinch, but then she realizes that I'm unarmed. She raises her gun. It's an assault rifle, an EX100, if I remember right. What else did I expect? The boss of P.I.D. has access to the best guns there are.

"Where's the bitch?" Charlotte's face is a mask of hatred.

"What are you talking about? I'm alone."

"Bullshit! I can hear the little tramp running."

"What was this blood fest back there all about?"

Charlotte adjusts her corset. "These are Stegner's people. The rat must have gotten wind of my expedition. He'll pay for this act of treason. I'll stuff him in the space cannon myself. Mark my words."

"Are we now killing each other for a change?"

Charlotte lowers her gun. "I need your help, Brick. We're still a team. The best team there is."

"Team?" I scoff.

"We're on the same side."

"I don't think so."

"We're Universals."

"Universals? Like the poor devils down there who've been just hacked to pieces? Is this your idea of unity?"

"Stegner's a threat to our unity. He's in cahoots with the enemy."

"Who is the enemy, Charlotte?"

"Are you joking?"

"I don't know what to think anymore."

"This little tramp has tried to turn you. You're acting like a stranger. But I'll bring you back into the fold."

I wave her off. "You're talking to the wrong man."

"Do you have any idea what this bitch plans to do? Do you realize what she needs these four keys for? She's just using you, that's what she does."

"What about you? Haven't you used me, too?"

"I put the Universal cause before everything else."

"Are you sure?"

"Brick, the bitch wants to restart the pioneer program."

"What if she does?"

"Don't you know what this means?"

I ignore her.

"It means," Charlotte continues, "that she'll destroy everything. New Berlin, our country, everything we've fought for."

"I don't know what I've been fighting for. When I think about it, I don't even know for whom."

"You're confused, Brick. I understand. Let's first go up into the tower to stop this bitch. We'll talk later."

I shake my head, no. "Too late, Charlotte." Zoe must have reached the door on Top-Level 10 by now. I look at Charlotte. "Do you know what I've come to understand at last?"

"Careful, Brick."

"I've come to understand..." I get up and spread my arms. "I'm a Colonial, Charlotte. I'm the enemy. I've been the enemy all along. A goddamn colonist, that's what I am."

"Stop talking like this!" Charlotte bangs her gun against the railing. "I need to go up there! With you or without you! Decide!"

"You know what, Charlotte? Go to hell!"

"Think it over."

"There's nothing to think about."

"Don't fuck up now, Brick."

"My mind is made up."

"If you're sure..." Charlotte points the assault rifle at me. "It's a pity. A real pity. I'm sorry that it has to end like this, Brick. I don't mind human beings. I really don't. Not like Tom. Tom hated humans. Oh, he hated your kind so much. I don't harbor ill feelings toward you people. As far as I'm concerned, humans, too, can be part of our community." Charlotte's finger curls around the trigger. "It's a real pity it has to end like this. I really think highly of you, Brick. Believe me. But the Community always comes first."

57

Forbidden Zone, Inside the TV Tower, Top-Level 5

We've faced death together and didn't let it have its way. Side by side, we've fought, suffered, and died. We gave everything we had, unbending, steadfast, and without ever faltering. For twenty long years. Remember. Don't you ever forget. But truth was that none of us remembered a thing. I wasn't able, the others weren't willing. Actually, we never really knew the name of the game we were playing. And we didn't know the target of our hatred either. This, at least, goes for the humans among us. But all of this is behind me now. A bullet will launch me on my journey. And this was it, I guess.

"Do we get to meet, at last, my little Solitaire?" Charlotte trains her gun on a point above my head. For a moment I'm confused. Someone's coming down the stairs. I turn. It's Zoe. Her eyes are fixed on Charlotte. "I'll take Brick up to the bridge now. And you… you leave us."

An ugly laugh from Charlotte. "Have you ever seen a baby like this?" She points her assault rifle directly at Zoe's heart. "Just think of the nice little holes it'll punch into your pretty body, sweetie-pie."

I move to shield Zoe with my body. "I hope you've brought enough ammo for both of us."

Charlotte raises her brows, her face a mask of surprise and contempt. "Do you have any idea who this creature is, who's standing behind you, Brick?"

"I know who's standing right in front of me. That's enough."

"It's between her and me. Get out of my way, Brick!"

"No!"

Charlotte adjusts her corset. "You stupid idiot! You really have no idea what's happening here. Am I right?"

"I'm sure you're about to enlighten me."

"Your little friend belongs to the Superiors, Brick."

"Superiors? Our betters? What's that supposed to be?"

"Humans like you are no more than animals to them. Like roaches you squash, when they get in your way."

"This doesn't make sense."

"How did she turn you, Brick?" Resentment contorts Charlotte's features.

"You'll never understand."

"Has this lying traitor fooled you into believing that humans like you will be treated as equals?"

"She told me about the rebellion."

"Rebellion? What rebellion? That's utter bullshit. What's there for Superiors to rebel against?"

"The mycelium."

"Mycelium?" Charlotte takes a step back. "That's her name for our holy Community?"

I nod, yes. "The mycelium doesn't tolerate dissent. It prevents individual growth and blocks progress."

"How pathetic, Brick. You start sounding like a parrot," Charlotte scoffs. "Who has fed you this gibberish? Well, I can guess, who."

"What do you stand for, Charlotte?"

"I stand for unity, Brick. I'm a Universal. Through and through."

"Unity..." I murmur.

For a moment, there is a sparkle in Charlotte's eyes. "Right, Brick. Unity. And you can be part of this Community. You still can."

"But there's something I simply don't understand. Do you know what I just can't get my head around? Where did this hatred against the Colonials come from?"

"Hatred?"

"Yes. What's your problem with us? We had no idea that this planet was already inhabited. We just wanted to settle down. Live in peace. Raise our families. We didn't come as enemies. The *Icarus* wasn't a battleship."

Charlotte eyes me skeptically, obviously weighing her words. "It wasn't about you people, Brick. It never was."

"So?"

"Our holy Unity is in jeopardy."

"Unity? What goddamn Unity are you talking about?"

"The only one that counts: The Unity of our planet. You humans have upset the time-honored balance. You have brought us war, dissent, and violence. You woke up the Solitairs."

Zoe steps in front of me. "Why are you still in this body?"

Charlotte's eyes are filled with disgust. "Well, well, well, we're talking again, aren't we?"

Zoe makes a move in Charlotte's direction. "Why haven't you left behind your human body a long time ago?"

"Do you think this body means anything to me? I'll return as soon as my work is done."

"What do you call yourself? Charlotte?" Zoe wipes a strand of hair off her face. "You know, Charlotte, I've never learned how to express emotions with my face or to interpret other people's feelings correctly. These things are difficult for me. Very difficult. Living in this body is not easy. But maybe it has already influenced my way of thinking more than I care to admit. Maybe I'm more human than I realize. The word humans use for it is 'gut feeling'. And now my gut feeling is telling me that you're lying."

"Bullshit!" Charlotte screams. "Unity... I want Unity! That's all I'm fighting for!"

"Why are you wearing this corset, then? Why do you use makeup, Charlotte? Why do you go through so much trouble, just to delay the decline of your human body?"

"I'll give you the only answer you deserve, traitor!" Charlotte's finger curls around the trigger.

58

Forbidden Zone, on the Bridge of the Colonist Platform New Berlin

Memories are like meandering whitewater streams. Sometimes I see myself sitting at the banks of River Spree. I have a date for a picnic. There are two wine glasses in front of me, one of them with lipstick on its rim. It's a solemn occasion, the eve of the big day. The day that will mark a farewell and a new beginning.

A pounding at the door yanks me from my thoughts. Charlotte doesn't give up so easily. She's always been the stubborn kind. But no matter how persistently she keeps on hammering away, the builders of New Berlin have done a good job in securing the bridge. Charlotte's wrath won't be enough to break down the steel door. I've never seen her so rattled. Maybe she can't give up control, because it makes her feel humiliated. She seemed to be surprised herself, when she fired the shot. Jealousy, revenge, despair, I don't know the exact reason why she went ballistic. Overwhelmed by her own emotions, Charlotte acted like a real human being. The much-trumpeted unity, die ideals of her holy community, all dissolved in a puff of gun smoke. I took advantage of her momentary confusion. I'm not proud of having hit a woman. But pride isn't the issue here. There is much more at stake.

Zoe sits in the captain's chair. She doesn't breathe and has no pulse. I've carried her all the way up here. Up the stairs inside the tower, five top-levels high, Charlotte in hot pursuit. Without her assault gun she had no way of stopping me. My ears still ring from her curses. Charlotte shot Zoe square in the heart. But the wound has stopped bleeding now, a brownish plug closing up the hole. When I look at Zoe, I'm sure that she isn't dead. And then, suddenly, it really happens. Without warning her carotid artery starts to throb. The beats are strong. Zoe's chest raises and falls. Three breaths later, Zoe opens her eyes and looks at me. "Your pupils are dilated, Brick."
I smile at her. "You're back."
"Why?"
"Charlotte only hit a fungal node, but fortunately you people have three of them. You're really a sturdy bunch. Chapeau."
"Why are your pupils widened, I mean?"
"Are they?"
"Not anymore. But they were a moment ago."
"I guess, it's... well, it was probably just a human reaction."
"And what was your message?"
"I'll tell you some other time."
Zoe looks toward the exit. "Who's hammering against the door?"
"Charlotte."
"Charlotte? You haven't killed her?"
"I've told you, I'm not a killer."
"Yes, you did."

I hold out the captain's key to her. "I already plugged the first three keys into their consoles. I think you deserve the honor of inserting the final one."

Zoe straightens. "We have to start the pioneer program. The others will be here soon."

"What happens, once you start the program?"

"The solar panels will unfold. Ground water will be pumped into the dry central canal."

"But won't the mycelium ocean come directly to New Berlin if the canal is flooded?"

"The water is brought up from deep down. It's filtered, reprocessed, and sterilized again and again in an eternal cycle."

"Sounds great."

"However, there's one more thing..." Zoe stops. If I didn't know better, I'd think that there's sadness reflected in her face.

"What's wrong?"

"I'll also put out the eternal fire on Museumsinsel."

"So? That's what you wanted to do all along."

"Right."

"What makes you so sad, then?"

"The blanket of smoke will dissipate. The sun, Brick, the sun will shine on New Berlin."

"Are you saying...?" The impact of our decision to initiate the pioneer program starts to dawn on me. "You told me all buildings and landmarks, yes, almost everything in New Berlin consists of fungus!"

"The fungus has formed the city."

"And the fungus can't survive in sunlight..."

"The fungus will wither away. It won't take long for the supporting framework to turn brittle."

"And then New Berlin, as we know it, will crumble to dust?"

Zoe nods, yes. "But it's the only way. A new beginning can only follow after destruction."

"Are you really sure that you want to start the program?"

"There is no other choice, Brick. I want us to live together. Colonists and Rebels. All of us. But without the mycelium."

59

Forbidden Zone, on the Bridge of the Colonist Platform New Berlin

The control panels are switched on, the displays are blinking and strobing, the fans of the computers emit a steady hum. In spite of all damages the bridge seems to be in working order. Zoe initiates the colonizing modules one by one. The keys of the captain and his officers allow her unlimited access to all systems of New Berlin. I sit at the console next to her, my fingers drumming a nervous tattoo on the table. My edginess doesn't escape Zoe, who looks in my direction. "What's wrong?" she asks.

"I just had an idea..."

"You're scrolling through the list of colonists. Why?"

I end the search program and return to the start screen. "Nine-hundred years, you said? We've really spent nine-hundred years in space?"

"That's what the files say."

"That's a long time. A real long time."

Zoe smiles in her very special way. "We need to look ahead, Brick. Not back into the past."

"Universals, Colonials, Rebels, Superiors. Nothing but names. In the end it all comes down to power and influence."

"The world we will build will be a better world."

"You really believe it, don't you?"

"With all my heart." Zoe touches her hand to the brownish plug that seals her chest wound.

"A better world..." I murmur. "I'm really curious what it will look like." I walk to the glass front and peer outside. New Berlin is hidden under a thick blanket of smoke. "What stops us from letting the sun shine bright over the city? The light will do all of us a lot of good."

Zoe walks up to me. "For a better world, Brick. I promise."

I nod, gazing into the distance. "Do you think there's still some wine around here?"

"What do you want wine for?"

"I'd like to invite you to a picnic at the banks of River Spree."

"A picnic?"

"We could watch the riverbed being flooded."

"You and I?"

"I've been there a lifetime ago, Zoe. On earth. At the banks of the real Spree."

"With... with a woman?"

I look into Zoe's eyes. "I've dreamed about it often, you know. About a picnic at the Spree. But in my dreams the woman next to me wasn't... she wasn't human."

"Do you think...?" Zoe reaches for my hand.

I frown. "Since when do you like to be touched?"

"Don't people touch when they like each other?"

"We Universals have always held hands, believe me. And what did it help us?"

"Not Universals and Rebels, Brick. A man and a woman are holding hands."

"A man and a woman. Sounds pretty good. Just one more thing..."

"What?"

"No fungus voodoo."

"Fungus voodoo?"

"No manipulations."

"Well, I think it's rather you manipulating me."

"Me?"

"I feel good when I'm with you, even though I don't know why."

"I feel the same way, Zoe. But I think I know the reason."

"How come?"

"You'd better find out yourself, I think."

"Do you like me holding your hand?"

"Yes, very much."

"I like it, too, Brick."

60

At the Bank of Spree Canal, One Week Later
(… a swish, then a click…)

We haven't invited these creatures, who call themselves humans. They came without being asked. The humans claim that they've come to colonize new worlds. The contraption they've landed with, the humans call a spaceship. The name of the spaceship is *Icarus*, they say, named after a man who tried to soar up into the skies. But his wings were made of wax and melted in the sun. The colonists' platforms have perforated our planet like spikes. Since that time the balance of our world has been upset.

I'm using the dictating machine I took from the traitor called Brick. My first impulse was to destroy his records. But even though this enemy of our community has succeeded in triggering the pioneer program, I've come to the conclusion that his words could help me to defeat the Colonials. The fight for New Berlin has just begun. It will be a long and bloody war, but in the end we Universals will prevail. Over and out. Charlotte Fleming.

To be continued…

A heartfelt thank you to all of you who have supported me during the publication of this thriller, first of all my wonderful crew: Ingo, Michael, Sylvia, Ilona, Janet, and my dear mother. In remembrance of my dear father, Fritz Krepinsky.

A very special thanks to my Lovelybooks circles! It's always a pleasure!

Once again I'm grateful to all my readers for their confidence in a free-lance author like me.

In memoriam Franziska Pigulla who read out my novel *Spreeblut* with so much passion.

Dear greetings to the staff of "Milch & Zucker", "Codos", "Boxi", "Kala", and all the other Berlin cafés, where I hung out to write. SomaFM Dronezone is and will always be the best background music while writing. Just listen in!

To share your questions, suggestions, and criticism, please write to: info@nichtdiewelt.de.

You can also contact me via Instagram or Facebook. Communicating with you means a lot to me. Your feedback is therefore very welcome.

Karsten Krepinsky

www.theworldbehindthewindow.com

More books by Karsten Krepinsky

Berlin 2039: The Reign Of Anarchy

Population has doubled within the last twenty years, leading to a living hell where poverty, crime, and claustrophobia rule. Those who can afford it, have withdrawn to the well-protected gated communities, while the police have left entire neighborhoods to their own devices. In these lawless blank spots the authorities use so-called pushers to maintain a level of constant unrest between Arab clans, Turkish gangs, and Chechen brotherhoods. They are mavericks, men and women outside the law, who only answer to their supervisors based in the LKA, which is short for Landeskriminalamt, the State Office of Criminal Investigation. This is the story of Hauke the Pusher and Detective Natasha…

The Attack Of The ISombies

Zombies have launched an attack on Berlin, slaughtering anyone who gets in their way. While politicians run for cover, a mismatched group of young outcasts stands up to the challenge…

A Tower Below The Sea

Six people, all up for a good party. They work for Global Companion, a multi-national corporation, and are now airlifted to a yacht anchored in the Atlantic. A one-week luxury vacation is awaiting the winners of the company sweepstakes. However, they are in for a tragic disappointment. A heavy storm forces the chopper's pilot to risk an emergency landing on a darkened offshore oil rig, whose crew seems to have gone AWOL. Pools of blood strongly point to gruesome happenings on board. Soon, the first brutal murder occurs. Who is behind it? And who will be slaughtered next? The only answer seems to be death, an evil force which shrouds this island made of steel like a blood-red veil …

The World Behind The Window
After a major catastrophe an entire country is without hope. A young man travels to the site of the disaster in the quest for a document that carries the promise of a better future.
The city is almost deserted. The few remaining inhabitants live in hiding in derelict buildings or in shelters deep below ground. Some of them seemed to be trapped in the city: a young woman, trying to save her brother. An old man, who cannot remember his past. An old guard, who cruises the streets at night. In the ruins of the city the young man again and again is confronted with the remnants of the Old Order. "Fear the smiling face of the angry man." What is the secret behind the writings on the walls? When the young man reaches the end of his journey, he has learned the truth about the city and about himself.

The author
Karsten Krepinsky is a German author and lives in Berlin. He holds a PhD in biology. When not working for a start-up company in the field of neurosciences, his passion is to write mystery, sci-fi, and horror novels. A great source of inspiration to Karsten is the vibrant city of Berlin.

The translator
Karin Dufner, holder of an M.A. in American literature, has been working as a translator of fiction since 1989, seeing herself as a wanderer between the English and the German language. Her bibliography encompasses around 400 titles. Her ivory tower is located in the Düsseldorf area, Germany.

The cover designer
Ingo Krepinsky is co-founder and manager of the Bremen, Germany based design agency Die Typonauten. He studied communication design at the University of the Arts Bremen and the University of Applied Sciences and Arts Hannover. He has won several design contests such as *iF communication design award*, *The German Design Award* (nominated) or *Stiftung Buchkunst* (best designed books). The design performance and font work of Die Typonauten are consistently presented in international journals. The foundry was selected as German independent type foundry for *Typography, Referenced—A Comprehensive Visual Guide to the Language, History, and Practice of Typography*, a publication of Rockport Publishers.